CW00793462

My Human Wife

Olympia Black

My Human Wife © 2024 by Olympia Black. All Rights Reserved.

All rights reserved. No part of this book may be reproduced in any form or by any electronic or mechanical means including information storage and retrieval systems, without permission in writing from the author. The only exception is by a reviewer, who may quote short excerpts in a review.

Cover designed by Rebecca Frank

This book is a work of fiction. Names, characters, places, and incidents either are products of the author's imagination or are used fictitiously. Any resemblance to actual persons, living or dead, events, or locales is entirely coincidental.

Printed in the United States of America

First Printing: February 2024

ISBN: 979-8-9903340-0-7

“Anything we can imagine about such other life forms is possible, of course. You could have psychotic civilizations, or decadent civilizations that have elevated pain to an aesthetic and might covet humans as gladiators or torture objects, or civilizations that might want us for zoos or scientific experimentation, or slaves or even food. While I am appreciably more optimistic, we just can't be sure what their motivations will be.”

Stanley Kubrick, Interview (1968)

Dear Readers

I have two important things I would like to highlight about this book.

First, the story of *My Human Wife* is told mainly by two characters, but I have chosen to use three slightly different writing styles by chapters. These are as follows:

- 'Gael,' the male main character written in first person present tense
- 'Lara,' the female main character written in first person present tense
- 'Kamos,' a supporting male character written in first person present tense
- 'Gael and Lara: Duet,' both main characters are written in first person present tense simultaneously and marked '*g.*' and '*l.*' for clarity.
- 'Kamos and Lara: Duet,' both main characters are written in first person present tense simultaneously and marked '*k.*' and '*l.*' for clarity.

I initially wrote this book for a male and female duet narration by Bridget and Jake Bordeaux which will be available on Audible from 2024, which is why I have numerous, clearly marked, duet chapters. I hope they prove to be just as moving in print as in audio.

Second, this book contains shocking scenes with aliens in intimate circumstances, as well as instances of, racism, Stockholm Syndrome, humiliation, miscommunication, dubious consent, slavery, alien abduction, voyeurism, and sex for physical gratification. Themes such as body count and Oedipus complex are also explored. All characters in this book are morally grey.

Be warned, I do not shy away from explicit encounters or highly emotional scenes. Unquestionably, my books are not for the faint of heart but are observations about the human condition.

Best wishes,

Olympia

Chapter 1

Lara

"No! For the love of the goddesses! You can't leave me here!" I scream as I run barefoot on the sharp stones. "I'm not a believer!"

The Intergalactic Court representative doesn't even turn around to acknowledge what he's done. And I watch as he gets into his transport and leaves me on this desolate rock with one building, a temple to the Fertility Goddess. But let's call it what it really is, a sex temple. A place for aliens to come to have interspecies sex legally. Only a small offering is required.

This is the last place in the galaxy I want to be.

Admitting temporary defeat, I sit down on the tainted steps. I'm pushed back and forth with the rhythm of aliens passing me by, going up and down the steps. Worshipers pass me like a discarded toy.

How did I get here?

Just two weeks ago I was the prized possession of my Uru master, a collector of rare species in the galaxy. I was covered in gold and preserved like a prized possession only to be taken out on special occasions. Important people traveled lightyears across the galaxy to see me.

And now, suddenly I'm here. Alone at one of the trashiest temples in the galaxy with nothing. The IGC took everything from me. My jewelry, my clothing, my leash. Anything that I could have sold for universal credits.

I'm not supposed to be here.

I look up at the sky for encouragement, but it isn't a sky at all. It's just a clear forcefield. The only thing separating this fornication temple from deep space. My throat tightens. I'm marooned on rock in the cold badlands of the galaxy.

What am I going to do?

It's obvious that the only way on or off is with a transport. How will I convince anyone to take me with them? What can I offer? Not much. I wonder if it'd be possible to steal someone's ship? I have a good translator and my master educated me in a few languages so I can read and speak.

Funny thing about translators, most ships block them, so it's impossible to steal ships from another species unless you can read and speak some of their language like a native. And that goes for weapons, locks, and most other important or useful things in the galaxy. The better universal translators become, the more advanced specific translator blockers evolve to keep other aliens out.

I eye the transports outside the temple. Most of them are Octopod and Agnorrian. I can read Agnorrian and I could fly an Agnorrian ship as long as it had autopilot. But where would I go? There's nowhere really safe for humans except Earth, but I don't even know where Earth is except that it's far out on one of the most outer arms of the Milky Way. Although, the chances that I can steal a transport, then a spaceship, and then get home are next to nil.

What do other humans do in the galaxy?

I know, most humans are owned. There are rumors of humans being traders and having their own ships. But what do I know about trading? Nothing. My skill set is to be sexually pleasing for tentacled aliens.

I only have myself to bargain with.

I try to be pragmatic. I try to push all my anxiety down. I straighten my shoulders and hold my head high, as if preparing to sell myself on these dirty stone steps. I mentally go over what I have to offer. I inspect myself and realize it's not just my feet that are filthy but my entire body. The gold paint that usually covers my skin has begun to chip off by the all hands that have touched me since my master's death.

I close my eyes for a few seconds, willing myself to let the wave of emotions pass through me. It doesn't work. My heart is beating so fast. I wonder if this is what a heart attack feels like. I feel wetness escape the corners of my eyes.

Am I going to die here with an alien over me? Death by alien sperm?

No. I can't.

I rest my head on the top of my knees and watch as gold flakes from my skin fall and then are swept away by alien appendages going to-and-fro on the filthy steps. No one pays any attention to me.

Seconds turn into minutes, and minutes into hours and all the while, I sit stunned by my predicament.

Suddenly from out of nowhere, a tentacled arm grabs me and I'm forced to look up. I follow the pain as the alien's circular suckers purposely pull on my delicate skin. My skin feels like it could be sucked off my bone completely.

"Obscene human! You've been sent here by the powerful Intergalactic Court judge Jin Kol. As such you are our *sacred* responsibility until you fulfill your duty to the Goddess of Fertility. I will not allow you to waste away like trash on the steps of this blessed temple."

I look up at a purple tentacled Uru nun and I suppress a laugh, *Sacred, I'm sure.* She has two small yellow eyes, two legs and eight tentacled appendages.

I ignore her for a moment as if she were an apparition. I'm not ready to accept this reality.

Clearly, she is not a phantom.

My head hits the stone step with a melon-like thud, and I feel my brain inside my skull bounce. I feel wet blood spilling from my head. I have no thoughts anymore. I'm a goldfish. I just watch alien feet, tentacles and shoes step over me, up and down. Suddenly, I feel my body being pulled over the uneven stones. I smile stupidly assuming I'll be pulled to my death. The pain in my head is overwhelming. I want to tell the nun it's a good thing she's killing me because I don't want to die from the toxin of some alien male's sperm. I'd much rather my life be ended by a female who hates me for being a human than a male for carnal curiosity pleasure.

I close my eyes with the expectation of the great rush of memories everyone says happens when you die. I anticipate seeing my parents again. I remember leaving for school and kissing my mother good-bye. 'Have a nice day,' she said. It wasn't a *nice* day. I was abducted and I never saw her again.

"Human! Open your eyes. This isn't a holiday. This is the Fertility Goddess's Temple, and you have a duty to perform."

I tentatively open one eye. I see a different nun. She's Agnorrian, meaning she has two arms, two legs, white hair, purple eyes and grey skin.

"What do I have to do to leave?" I ask sitting up and touching my head. There's dried blood on my face and in my hair. I look around, this looks like a rundown infirmary from the last century.

"Just like everyone else who enters this temple, you must pay homage to the Fertility Goddess with a male and then you may leave."

"How do I do that?" I know the answer to this question. Everyone in the galaxy knows the answer to this question but I must ask it anyway just to make sure what I heard isn't propaganda.

"You stand in the female offering place and present yourself to males. If one of them chooses you, they'll make a donation to the temple. Then you'll have sex in one of the alter rooms before the Fertility Goddess's eyes. When the nuns and the goddess are satisfied with your donation then you are free to go."

"What if I don't want to have sex with anyone?"

"Then you must remain here as a servant of the goddess forever."

My eyes meet the nun's purple ones. "Is that why you're here?"

"That's none of your business. And don't even think about escape. We have no transport. Supply ships only come once a week and those are piloted by AI who are programmed to kill anyone who tries to board their ships."

"You assume too much, Nun..."

"Oh human, I've been here a long time. You'd be a fool *not* to think about escape. I thought about it all the time when I first arrived. You've already met our sadistic abbess, and she'd be bearable if it wasn't for all the abuse and death here."

"Have you tried to escape?"

"It's impossible. My advice to you is to have sex and leave as soon as you can. Once you become a nun..." she makes the Agnorrian gesture of her fist hitting her palm meaning you might as well be dead.

"Sex with any of these males might kill me."

"An Octopod won't kill you."

I make a face of disgust. "I might die from the memory."

"I know," she agrees. "And they can be brutal with humans, but maybe you'll get lucky. I suggest you pray." Then the nun gets out a tablet. "Now I have to ask you some questions since temporary guardianship has been passed from the IGC judge to the Fertility Goddess's Temple."

"I don't need guardianship. Humans are free now. It's galactic law."

"Unfortunately, as a human who has been owned you do need someone with citizenship to speak for you and to set you free." She makes fun of me by pretending to look around the dark stone room. "Is there someone here who is an IGC citizen who will vouch for you? No? I didn't think so. You are without galactic citizenship and therefore without a mouth to claim your freedom. It's ironic how galactic laws are made so that no one who really needs them can actually benefit from them. Funny that."

I'm irritated but I don't issue a rebuttal. She is correct after all. I am, for all intents purposes, stateless in the galaxy meaning that I'm at the mercy of the IGC and for now the nuns in this dirty temple. My master died before setting me free. But I know he would never have set me free. Then the IGC judge sent me here instead of setting me free. He could have but he didn't. And now the nuns own me and it doesn't look like they have any intention of setting me free until I risk my life having sex with an alien. But if I can look on the bright side, at least there seems to be a way out of here.

"But I can leave after I pay my respects to the goddess?" I ask to make sure I'd be risking my life for my freedom.

The nun looks up from the tablet surprised. “Isn’t that what I just said two minutes ago? Are you stupid or something?”

“Maybe I am.”

The nun bobs her head, an Agnorrian trait when they think someone or something is ridiculous, then asks me, “First question, when did you come to live with your former master?”

“I’ve already answered all of these questions.”

“Oh yes, the IGC file. We’d be fools to accept all their records as ‘accurate.’ Everyone in the galaxy keeps their own records and then later if they match up with the IGC records then happy days for everyone. Now, where was I?” she looks at the tablet. “When were you bought by your previous master?”

“About eight galactic years ago.” My master would mark the day of my entrance into his menagerie with a gift for me. It was never anything I wanted but jewelry and trinkets I wish I still had to bribe my way out of here.

“Where?”

“Gala Station.”

“You’re sure?”

“No one sold at Gala will ever forget the place. I’m quite sure.”

“And before Gala?”

“Earth.”

“You’re sure?”

I give her the side eye. “Yes, I am sure. It was Earth. I was eight Earth years old when I was taken.”

“Abducted?”

"Abducted, lured, whatever you want to call it. I definitely didn't look at those disgusting green aliens and say, 'Take me with you away from my life with my loving parents.'"

"By whom?"

"The Dulu of course. Why would you even ask?"

"Always the Dulu, those little green buggers," she says under her breath. "And how long did you remain with them?"

"Not long. A few weeks."

"How long were you at Gala?"

"Seven days."

"You're sure?"

"The Octopods that sold us fed us once a day and we fought over the food. It was a spectacle for potential buyers. So, yes, I am sure. It was seven days of hell."

The nun bites her purple lip. "What happens there is a stain on the reputation of all the good people in the galaxy."

"It's more than a stain," I say. "Those seven days I endured at Gala were worse than my eight combined galactic years as an exhibit in a menagerie."

She clears her throat and takes on a professional tone, "And then you went straight into captivity with Lord Juo of the Uru Tribe?"

"Yes."

She pauses and looks me up and down, slowly scrutinizing my body. "Do you know why he covered you in gold?"

"He said it was because it made me easier on the eyes."

"And so it does. Your pale skin looks sickly. Are you ill? Your medical records and from what I can see with my scanner here report you as healthy."

"This is the natural color of my skin, I'm not sick."

"Well not everyone in the galaxy can be born beautiful," the nun says just as much to herself as to me. "What are your skills?"

"I can be pleasing." We are speaking Agnorrian and this phrase means 'I am an entertainer,' but Agnorrian doesn't have the word as a profession because only slaves entertain. Agnorrians go to extreme lengths to try and prove to the rest of the galaxy they have no slaves. Which is true, they just have a lot of people who "are pleasing" and are unable to make any choices for themselves.

"Do you play an instrument or speak any languages besides Agnorrian?"

"I speak my human language, Uru, and a few others."

"Imperial?"

"No."

"That's odd."

"Lord Juo was under the impression that if I learned Imperial I'd be taken in by their religion and suffer brain damage."

"Well, Imperials and humans are the same species. It's a fair precaution. You won't see any Imperials here. Wrong side of the galaxy."

"I hadn't even thought about it."

"Play an instrument?"

I name off a few instruments I learned to play to please my master, "And I can sing."

"Did you do a lot of singing for your master?"

"Yes."

"Sex?"

"When asked."

"Were you compliant?"

"I rarely had reason not to be. Are you finished?"

"You're quite feisty for a human who was kept as part of a menagerie." Then she puts the tablet down. "Well Lara from Earth, I think it's time you presented yourself. You'll have a better chance of finding a male while you still have some gold paint on you. Unfortunately, there's not really a market for pale human kink here. Make sure you open your eyes wide. No one is put off by green eyes. You can thank the goddesses for those and maybe some desperate male will take pity on you. And my last piece of advice if you think a male might want you, sing a song. It's so rare we hear someone actually able to sing. None of the males that visit here are wealthy enough to have ever seen a professional singer, it might be the only thing that saves you."

Although my master doted on me, I know that most aliens on this side of the galaxy find my appearance repulsive. Visitors to Lord Juo's menagerie never hid their reactions when I was presented as 'the human woman' from his collection. Sometimes I would be presented already painted gold and other times he would allow his special visitors to paint me themselves. I let that memory slip away as I follow the white-haired nun into the massive temple.

I hear worshippers before we reach the open dome. Once inside the main temple, the dark air fills with the sweet smell of incense. My eyes are drawn up and a massive statue of who I suppose is the Goddess of Fertility is looking down at me with large painted stone eyes. She's like the Uru nun who hit me on the stairs outside but with enormous carved stone tentacles reaching all around the immense temple walls, inside every sucker is a small red candle. Above the statue is a round opening where I can see into space. Nothing but stars. *My freedom if I don't die here.*

"You know which alien males will poison you with their sperm?"

"I didn't think females had a choice in who chose them?"

"Females don't but you can hide when you see the poisonous ones coming. Just don't let the abbess see you. Now, go stand over there with the other females." She points to an area under one of the Fertility Goddess's outstretched tentacles, the candles in the suckers casting strange shadows on the space. As I approach, I notice there are about 20 other alien females in the offering area, but not one looks remotely humanoid. They all move away from me as I enter. I bow to them and say in Agnorrian which is the lingua franca in this part of the galaxy, "Bless us all." The other females just stare at me as it's a shock I can speak unaccented Agnorrian. There's a nasty rumor that humans aren't fully sentient and can only learn a few words and sentences, but not have complex thoughts. I let this roll off my back. Maybe they are scared to be here too. No lucky female ends up at the sex temple. Before the nun walks away I ask, "What happens if I don't get chosen?"

"Pray to the goddess you do. Remember open those green eyes as wide as possible."

I stand obediently with the other females. As the hours pass, it seems like everyone is being chosen except for me. The most beautiful tentacled females and the wealthiest are gone in seconds, the latter having paid for their lovers to come claim them and the former being followed by would-be suitors. Out of boredom I try to strike up a conversation with some of the other females in the offering box, but they have no time to talk to me. I hear the word, 'human' on their lips like a curse so I decide to sit down and have a break from offering myself. I keep a lookout for the abbess though, no doubt she'd beat me again for sitting and I know it's not acceptable as none of the other females are sitting, despite being noticeably exhausted.

There's no way to tell time as there's no sun or reference point, but I assume it's late as the temple is almost empty except for some nuns. I'm the only female in the offering area now. A few males saunter in take one look at me and then quickly leave. With nothing else to do, I lie down in the offering area on the cold stone floor and look up at the Fertility Goddess. I question her, "Why don't you help me?"

Out of nowhere, a purple tentacle slaps me hard across the face. I feel my teeth bite into the flesh of my mouth. I wipe the blood from my mouth and look up. It's the Uru abbess who slammed my head against the steps earlier.

"You should be grateful human." She grabs my arm roughly with another tentacle dragging me to my feet. "You're lucky to be here. If I had been that judge I would've sent you directly to Gala. The Fertility Goddess doesn't even see you because you're human, not worth her time, not sentient. You need a master."

"I need a medic," I reply calmly.

"Only one visit to the infirmary a day and you've already used your visit."

"Why not just let me go? Say I escaped."

"I'm not going to do *you* a favor at my expense. You will stay here, and you will try to find a male who will accept your filthy human flesh. Only then can you leave and go back to the IGC."

"Go back to the IGC? What? I thought I'd be free if I paid homage to the Fertility Goddess."

"Oh you foolish human female. This is just a stopgap for the IGC judge until he figures out what to do with you. And my guess is he assumes it'll take you years for a male to pay homage with you which is why he sent you here in the first place. He can't legally kill you and he doesn't want to sell you because now it's against the law, but he's not going to set you free or he would've already done it. And that's why I'm so annoyed. You're going to be with us forever and I never wanted a human pet. But if you're going to remain, I'm going to train you to be obedient if it's the last thing I do."

Chapter 2

Gael

"You won't believe this," my first officer says from his station.

I look up from my console on the bridge. It's late and I'm not in the mood to listen to anymore galactic gossip which my first officer is prone to repeat.

"A human woman, age 26 Earth years, has been dropped at the Fertility Temple by the IGC."

This piques my interest.

My first officer transfers information over to my console. It's a copy of an official IGC transferal of guardianship. It reads.

Status Pending: The human named Lara now is under the temporary guardianship of the Fertility Goddess's Holy Nuns as of Imperial Year 4th day of the 28th week of the year 18403 signed by the IGC official Jin Kol.

. . .

"Authenticity?"

"Verified. She was left there a few days ago. I'm bringing up the feed from the temple now." I look at my console again. Images from inside the Fertility Temple are sweeping past. On the sidebar is a list of alien life signs. I see one human. I touch the icon and see her. A blurry version of a blonde-haired human somewhat covered in gold paint appears on the screen.

"Should we pay the extra UCs for the sharpened image?"

I check the cost. "No. It's not worth it."

I bring up information about Jin Kol. He's Uru, of course, as are most of the IGC on that side of the galaxy, and look here, he's a devout believer in the goddesses. "It's a stopgap." As soon as I say it a plan blooms in my mind. I make eye contact with my first officer. "Set in a course. What is it? A few jumps?"

"It's completely out of our way and she's just one human woman who cannot be returned to Earth. She has to be a casualty for our greater cause. I only mentioned it because it was odd."

"She's not just any human woman. She was owned by Lord Juo of the Uru Tribe. I bet that she knows a lot about the galaxy's politics and would be more than willing to join us if we freed her from the nuns' guardianship."

"Or she could just have been a sex pet," my first officer says, using his own UCs to pay for the enhanced images from the Fertility Goddess's Temple.

I can't keep my eyes off the screen. Lara from Earth is still somewhat covered in gold paint. She is wearing a skimpy gold dress that shows off all of her curves. Her feet are bare and bloody and her long blonde hair a mess. But she is still incredibly attractive. "Even if she's mute, she still could be an asset. Set in a course."

I look up as my first officer joins me in the conference room. I've spent the last hour working on a plan to steal a teleportation suit prototype. Our first attempts have failed and I'm ready for a break. So, when my first officer enters I'm grateful for the interruption.

"My UCs have bought a free one-time viewing of an offering from the Fertility Temple in real time. Do you want to watch it?"

"Do we know what kind of species are involved?"

"No."

"We better watch a little just to make sure it's not our human. I don't want to go to the temple only to discover she's already left."

Seo sits down next to me and turns on the main viewer. It shows a humble stone room with a statue of the Fertility Goddess in the corner. Her jeweled eyes watching everything. The room is empty for a few minutes.

"I guess this is what you get for only paying the minimum price, an invisible show."

"The message said it might take a few minutes as all of this is happening in real time."

A few minutes later a female Uru, a tentacled humanoid with yellow eyes, and an Agnorrian enter.

"This is going to be interesting." Agnorrians have two sets of genitalia. Two penises and two vaginas. Uru males have only one hectocotylus that detaches to complete the sexual act.

"Why would he choose an Uru?" Seo asks.

"Both species like it when the penis breaks off inside of them. What other species find sexy..." I trail off as we watch. The silver haired purple Agnorrian begins stripping off the Uru female's clothing and toying with her tentacled arms. She begins leaving round dark purple sucker marks all over the Agnorrian's chest. He in turn massages her three small breasts all with yellow nipples standing to attention. I've seen images of naked Uru females, but to watch one in action is intriguing. In turn the female pulls down the Agnorrian's trousers to reveal two fully erect penises.

"I can't believe those are going to break off inside of her."

"I can't believe she'd want that."

"I can't believe we're *still* watching this. It's not our human."

"I can't look away. Although I might want to burn my eyes out afterwards."

The Uru female is enveloping the Agnorrian with her eight tentacled arms and if I didn't know there was something sexual going on I'd think the Agnorrian was being attacked to be eaten. This goes on for a few minutes and then the tables turn and the Agnorrian, no doubt using the mental abilities that most Agnorrians possess, pins all of the Uru female's tentacles to the dirty wet stone floor. He then begins breathing heavily all over her body which is equivalent to kisses for Imperial people, or so I've been told. Once he reaches her vagina, which is also her anus, he positions himself and inserts one of his penises. She's struggling against his mind control, but not saying 'no' so clearly, she just wants to be a more active participant.

"Do you think he can have sex with her and keep her down at the same time?"

"No. Not for both of his penises," I say not taking my eyes off the screen.

"Five UCs says the Agnorrian succeeds in keeping her down."

"And I say, the Uru female will break free before he finishes."

We continue watching with more enthusiasm now. The Agnorrian is plunging his organ in and out of the Uru and she's still writhing against his mind control. When the Agnorrian's first penis snaps off with a loud pop inside of the Uru's one hole, my first officer and I physically pull back with a start.

"I never need to see that again."

"Ugh, it just came off." I put my hand down to touch my own genitalia to make sure it's still there. "And the sound. I'll never unhear that 'pop.'"

Seo swallows hard and checks the status of his own genitalia as well.

But fascination gets the better of us and we continue watching. Without any break the Agnorrian gets into position with his second penis.

"Apparently Agnorrians don't need a refractory period between penises."

"Something I thought I'd never consider."

"He's not going to put it into the same hole, is he? Look his other one is already stuck in there and you can see it wiggling around as if it's trying to climb up further."

"Where else is it going to go? Uru's don't have two vaginas or even a separation between anus and vagina. It's all one hole."

"Her mouth?"

"His penis has spikes on it to make sure it stays put. She'd die."

"Can he even fit another penis in her hole? It doesn't look like it."

The Agnorrian begins, but it's obvious he's exhausted and it's a tight fit with his other penis still lodged firmly in her vagina. As minutes pass, it's clear, the Uru female is gaining more strength. Just as his second organ breaks off with a loud 'pop' the female regains all of her control with such force that I think she might have only been *pretending* to be controlled. With lightning speed, she sits up and twists off the Agnorrian's head. Silver hair and a mass of purple blood go flying across the room. And the Uru female pushes the headless Agnorrian male to the floor.

Again, we both recoil in disgust.

After a minute I say, "I didn't expect that."

We both watch as nuns enter the stone room with ancient cleaning devices. They also bring in some of the females from the offering place to help them. The human Lara also enters. She begins to retch upon entering.

"I don't think we're going to have any problems convincing Lara to join us."

"Not if *this* is a common occurrence. I can't even imagine the pungent smell of alien sex and death in that room."

"Now we know why those rooms look so dirty."

I take a transport to the temple. It's late and I'm one of the only visitors judging by the transports, or lack thereof. I begin walking towards the large black monstrosity. It's always night here. *This is a sinner's place,* I think, not because I'm terribly religious, I'm just waiting for the goddesses to show me they really exist, but because I don't need to be religious to know when a place reeks of bad deeds and sorrow.

I walk through the massive iron doors. Before I even pass the threshold, I can smell interspecies sex, incense and non-humanoid aliens, the kinds of aliens that produce mucus to slide along the stones. I briefly cover my nose as I walk further. This isn't a safe place for a human or an Imperial. Neither of us should be here. I touch the top of my gun for reassurance and continue walking forward. The temple is dark and only lit by candlelight. I doubt any human can see well here. Although, this is probably the one-time when being blind in the dark is an advantage.

I reach the female offering area and Lara is the only one there as if she has been waiting for me. I don't believe in fate, but I do believe in luck. And sometimes it plays out in my favor. I smile thinking about my next move.

She's asleep. It's only now that I realize that in all my scheming, I hadn't thought about what I'm actually going to say to her.

I consider just picking her up and walking out, she looks so peaceful sleeping, but I must give her a choice even if I know that she will most likely agree. *What human would want to wait out death here?*

Chapter 3

Gael and Lara

{Duet}

g. "Lara from Earth," I begin but stop when she opens her eyes and we make eye contact. She has the most beautiful big green eyes that weren't noticeable in the temple's feed and I lose my train of thought as she gets up and walks over to stand in front of me. The top of her head barely reaches my shoulder.

l. "Are you Imperial?" I eye this striking grey man up and down. If it weren't for his skin color, he could be human. He's tall and has long wavy black hair that's cut in a fashionable way to show off his strong jaw and handsome face. His clothing looks like it's painted on his muscular body and he has some tattoos on his arms, but I don't recognize the symbols and he's armed with a large gun.

g. "Half Imperial. My mother was kept as a human pet."

l. "I was told Imperials never come here. Are you here to buy me for sex? To pay homage to the Fertility Goddess?" I look up at the massive statue and half wonder if she's real and has answered my call.

g. "Not exactly. I have a proposition for you."

l. "If it means I get to leave this place, my answer is 'yes.'"

g. "You've not even heard it. You may prefer to stay where you are."

l. "Look around. Do you think I want to remain here? I'm safer with you than all these males who might inadvertently poison me with sex. And you probably want me to be your pet which I've heard isn't a bad position for a human."

g. "No, no.." she touches my arm and interrupts me.

l. "Are you speaking English?" I wonder if I'm still dreaming but his arm feels real enough.

g. "I've been speaking English this whole time, haven't I?" *Is she delusional?*

l. "I've not conversed in English in such a long time I didn't even realize you were speaking my native language at first. Did your mother speak English?"

g. "Yes. We can talk about it later if you take me up on my offer. Time is a constraint at the moment..."

l. "I already said 'yes.'"

g. "For my own peace of mind, let me present the offer to you."

l. "Fine. Go ahead. My answer will still be 'yes.'"

g. "My name is Gael..."

l. "Gael the Returner? Leader of Terra Ka?"

g. "You've heard of me?"

l. "Are you joking? Of course. You're a myth spoken in whispers by every slave in the galaxy. Half human but looks Imperial and is determined to free humans. Have you come here to save me? Are you going to take me back to Earth?"

g. My heart breaks for her, I wish I could take her home. "I hate to disappoint you. I've come here to ask you to join our cause. I need you to use your skills to steal something for me. One mission and then you can go where you want."

l. "*Me* help *you*?" I point to my chest to make sure I heard this correctly.

g. "Do you agree?"

l. "Yes. I don't want to stay in this place a minute longer. Now let's get the tribute over with. You have to pay that nun..."

g. "I'm not going to pay to have sex with you that's recorded for some sadistic Uru nuns' pleasure."

l. "They record it?"

g. "Yes, and they sell it across the galaxy too. Come on."

Chapter 4

Lara

Have I fallen into a coma? It's way too much to believe that Gael the Returner has come to save me. I wonder if the abbess has hit my head against the stone floor again. It doesn't matter. I don't feel any pain, only a tingling between my legs and a tightness in my stomach. Perhaps I'm dying from toxic sex with an alien and if this is death then it's a good one.

Gael is holding my hand in his as we run together towards the temple doors that are now closing with the worst creaking noises that sound like an animal dying. It makes me run as fast as I can.

But it's not enough. Gael picks me up as if I weigh nothing and sprints for the door, but it closes before we can escape.

My dream is turning into a nightmare. The abbess is walking towards us with a look of satisfaction on her face. "You can't just come in here and steal, Imperial pirate."

"I'm not a believer," Gael says as if they were all having a civilized conversation about religion.

"Blasphemy. You will be a believer and you will pay homage to the Fertility Goddess. Five-hundred UCs for this human."

"As the goddesses abandoned me a long time ago, I'm not worried about their wrath for not paying."

"I choose him," I say in Uru, the abbess's native tongue hoping that might make a difference. The word 'choose' holds greater significance in their language.

Her yellow eyes meet mine. "Are you sure?"

I don't break eye contact, but I feel like I'm agreeing to more than just sex for the Fertility Goddess. But I don't back down. "Yes. I *choose* Gael the Returner."

The nun smiles deviously. "Well then, in that case, I grant you your freedom and I grant you *Gael the Returner*."

I think I've won something but when I look over at Gael his face looks ashen. I mouth the word, 'What?' in English but he doesn't acknowledge my question.

"Oh, the stupid human doesn't even know what she's done," the abbess laughs. "This is priceless."

"What have I done?"

"You've agreed to marry this man."

"No, I haven't."

The nun can hardly stop laughing to explain.

"Gael? Tell her she's losing her mind. I agreed to sex."

"Through my translator that's not what you said. You said 'marry.'"

"At Lord Juo's males often said they *chose* me in that formal way."

"It's a practice with prostitutes," the abbess tells me. "So males don't anger the goddesses and Uru society can say we don't have filles de joie. I'd feel sorry for you if you were just any human, but I don't want you here. And this is the only way I can get rid of you permanently."

"But you said if I paid homage to the goddess I'd go back to the IGC. I can pay homage with this man and leave."

"That was before I received this message." The abbess shows us a message from the desk of IGC Judge Jin Kol, Uru Tribe.

Status Resolved: The human named Lara now is an apprentice nun under the permanent guardianship of the Fertility Goddess's Holy Nuns as of Imperial Year 8th day of the 28th week of the year 18403 signed by the IGC official Jin Kol.

"Why would the IGC do that?" I ask.

"It doesn't matter now. You're not staying here. You've agreed to marry this criminal. Let's do this so I can be free of you." The abbess looks at Gael. "One UC if you please. You must still pay this temple its due."

"But he didn't agree," I protest.

"Ignorance doesn't change what you promised, human."

Chapter 5

Gael

I'm trying to think of ways to get out of this. With humans being in this legal limbo, what Lara said is binding if her guardian agrees. And clearly her guardian agrees wholeheartedly. As a man, unless I've shown severe unwillingness to enter into this union I can't refuse because legally she is free to decide. The only way out would be to not become sexually aroused during our homage to the goddess, but that would be impossible. Lara is the embodiment of the perfect woman, even dirty as she is now. I find everything about her attractive, the curve of her hips, her ample breasts and of course her human pink lips. I'm sure her tongue and clit are cherry-colored too. I'm aroused just thinking about it. And it's been over a year since I've touched a woman so there's no question if I can fulfill the marriage ceremony.

But her ignorance of the galaxy is tragic. She doesn't even know what she's done, and I won't tell her the extent of it anytime soon. I don't want to give her anything else to worry about. "This is binding," I say evenly. I get out my IC and transfer one UC to the temple. I look over to Lara who is shocked. I take her small hand in mine. "The sooner this is over the sooner we can leave."

The abbess, more than happy with the arrangement, smiles smugly. "Gael the Returner, Outcast of the Alliance Empire, Commander of Terra Ka, do you accept Lara from Earth, Ward of the Fertility Temple, formerly owned by Lord Juo of the Uru Tribe, to be your wife?"

"I accept Lara's offer," I say purposely using English.

"You are married," the abbess decrees as if this is some kind of love match and she the matchmaker. I can't help but give her a scathing look, but she ignores me.

"Don't I have to say something?" Lara asks.

I'm surprised by her question but before I can answer her, the abbess explains, "You already asked him in my presence. I'm anointed by the Fertility Goddess to oversee marriages."

"If I wasn't already an atheist, hearing that *you,* the nastiest of nuns, were 'anointed' by the goddesses to oversee matches, that would have instantly made me one," Lara says.

The abbess tries to take a swing at her with two of her largest tentacles, but I put my arm up to block her. "Hey now, that's my wife you grubby little Uru. Now let's get this show on the road as my mother used to say."

I don't know if it was my last comment or that I blocked Lara from being struck but she gives me an appreciative look. Maybe this is all going to be okay. It's not the way I planned it, but sometimes reality is better than expectations.

The abbess leads us into a dark room and I protest, "Humans can't see in the dark."

"Pity this is our best room." The abbess then leads us into another room. The stench is unbearable and this time it's Lara who objects.

"Not here, this is where that Agnorrian died."

I look around and recognize the room. The memory of the pop of his penis and then his head coming off plays through my mind.

We are then shown to a third room. It's very small and lit only by a few candles. There's no furniture to speak of and the stone floor is stained, but it only smells of incense and wet, no death. "Fine," I say. "Now leave."

The abbess departs but it doesn't matter. We are being watched by her and many others on the temple's live feed. I don't let go of Lara's hand, but instead pull her closer to me. She's standing stiff as if she's nervous.

Chapter 6

Gael and Lara

{Duet}

g. "We could try to escape another way, but the problem is we are being watched," I say, purposely speaking English with her. Most people in the galaxy don't have a translator for it because of the discrimination against humans. If people understood humans, it'd be much more difficult to say they are meant to be pets.

l. "That's not it. I can turn my mind off for the physical part."

g. "That's reassuring," I reply although my pride is hurt a little. But I remind myself of the life she has lived, it must have been a necessity for survival to not think about what's happening to her body while aliens had their way with her.

l. "The thing is, I've never had actual sex."

g. I don't know what to say. It takes me a minute to process this. "But you were kept in a menagerie. You just said when males wanted to be with you..."

l. "Yes, all that is true, but none of the males were ever humanoid like you. They didn't have the correct genitalia. They all had appendages that would kill me if they orgasmed and broke off inside of me, and my master took great care to keep his possessions healthy."

g. Oh goddesses, this is bad luck, isn't it? I stroke her long blonde hair in sympathy as I think. How am I going to do this in this dirty room with no furniture? I thought she was an expert, and I would be the one outclassed. Now, everything I think of saying sounds insulting.

l. I can't read his face. Maybe he doesn't want to touch me now realizing the kind of aliens that have used me for their carnal curiosities. I don't know what to say. I wish I'd never told him the truth. I know the basics of how humans do it. I decide to take matters into my own hands. I remove my gold dress slowly. And just like with every male his pupils dilate and fill with desire. Then I begin undressing him.

g. I need to stop her, but I can't. She is the most alluring creature and I'm already aching for sex. Although her body is half covered with gold and the other half dirt, and she has no jewelry which I assume was confiscated by the IGC or these nuns, she still is exquisite. Her breasts are full and her pink nipples sit high and taut. The blonde hair between her legs is intoxicating to me as I can already imagine more of her seductive scent culminating there. And she's more than willing, she's inviting me into her. Her hands are like silk caressing me as she removes my clothing. When she gets to my gun, we make eye contact. I take it in my hand wordlessly so it's out of the way and she doesn't give it another thought. She's either the bravest or the most foolish woman in the galaxy. As she begins to pull down my trousers, my erect penis springs out and she stops momentarily.

l. I hadn't expected him to be already aroused nor for him to have ridges across the top of his organ. *Are humans and Imperial men always aroused?* I don't know. Perhaps this will go much faster so that I don't have to lather any tentacles up. I curiously run my fingers over his ridges and he takes a deep breath. I pull his trousers all the way down and then turn and bend over showing him my vagina. When nothing happens, I put his free hand on my hip to indicate he can enter me.

g. A lesser man would have just entered her. But I am not a lesser man. Even in this strange situation, I want this to be a good memory for us both. "Turn around, Lara," I say my voice gruff with want. She stands up and obeys me. It pains me that I find her obedience attractive too. "I'm going to kiss you first. You do know what a kiss is?"

l. "I have seen it."

g. "But you've never been kissed?"

l. "Never. I've only ever had male tentacles shoved in my mouth."

g. "Let me be the first man to kiss you properly then," I say and lean down and touch my lips to hers. I can feel her tremble a little, so I steady her with my hand on her chin. She tries to pull back, but I keep her lips on mine. Slowly easing her into this kiss. I can taste blood in her mouth as my tongue enters. If this were any other situation I would draw back and ask her if she were okay, but that will have to wait. She could have easily bit her tongue or anything else in this place.

l. I didn't think Gael touching me, his lips to mine, would feel any differently than tentacled males putting their appendages all over me, but this feels incredibly different. He's awakened my body to my humanness. It's as if it has been turned off my entire life until now and now my body recognizes him as the same species and is willing. I want to reciprocate but I'm frozen with the realization I want this so much I'm afraid to do something wrong. When he puts his hand so gently on my chin, I feel things in my body I've never felt before. Is this what sexual desire feels like?

g. I reluctantly pull back. "I must put my gun down, at some point, but when I do, we will have to be quick. I'm sorry I didn't imagine..." I trail off. I didn't dream I'd be having sex with a woman who's never actually been with a man of her own species in a room with no furniture. Oh, and to add to that, my wife. My wife. *My human wife.* She looks up at me. Her green eyes filled with want and my worries about everything vanish. This is here and now. I won't rush this and most likely we won't be murdered, but that's only because this debaucherous temple is so far away from all my enemies that even if they happened to be watching on the live feed, they couldn't get here fast enough.

l. "You can hold your gun and have sex, can't you?"

g. "I'm not going to let your exquisite body touch anything in here. I'm going to hold you."

l. I want to tell him that he could enter me from behind, but I don't. I want him to hold me. I want him to touch me like I mean something. I watch him as he sets down his gun on the dirty floor and I expect him to immediately pick me up, but he doesn't. His hands cup my face and our eyes meet. His green eyes are hypnotic.

g. "Now," I say, and I lean in to lightly kiss her lips again. She's more relaxed now and kisses me back in a simple way. I take her modest kisses and then move my hands down to her neck, her shoulders, her back. I draw her closer to me so that her soft naked body is against mine. The crush of her breasts against my chest feels amazing. I hold her even tighter to me and plunge my tongue into her mouth. The coppery blood taste is mostly gone replaced with her. Replaced with us.

l. I've never felt this before. This erotic synergy between myself and another. My body takes complete control when he pulls me against his hard naked body. His large sex against my thigh pulsating with his desire. Once his hand touches one of my nipples I can't help but let out a moan of pleasure, which in turn pleases Gael. If this is what desire is supposed to feel like then why did all those Uru males want to touch me? What pleasure could they have derived from it if the desire was not reciprocated? I don't want to think of any of that now, but the stark contrast of my life before Gael touched me two minutes ago and now is somewhat intertwined because so many questions I had about eroticism just became clear.

g. I push back some of her hair from her ear. Pull her earlobe into my mouth and then say, "Don't think." I can tell something is bothering her. My mind screams out, *because she's a virgin to a humanoid*. And at the same time has been touched by how many alien males with tentacles not of her choosing? I try not to think about the latter. Only because I feel sadness for her.

l. His hot breath on my ear sends cold shivers up and down my body. I hold his mouth to my ear, grabbing some of his black hair in my fist. "Tell me more." I not only enjoy his mouth there but I also relish the sound of him speaking English to me. This is a fantasy I didn't even know I had until now.

g. I can talk dirty to her, of course I can, I'm half Imperial, after all. But I don't think she wants to hear what most free women in the galaxy like. So instead of making her submit to me, which is what Imperial women want, I say, "I'm honored you chose me." It's only after I say the words that I realize that I'm not lying.

l. "Say it again." His tongue enters my ear and I clinch my thighs together. I've never felt like this.

g. "I'm honored you chose me, Lara," I say as I move one hand between her legs and another to cup her backside. I begin moving my finger lightly over her clit. When she comes close to orgasm I break our kiss, get down on my knees and pull her needily to my mouth. I suck hard and hold her close. Her sounds of pleasure and her muscles tensing make me almost come myself. I must release inside of her or this won't be legal. I will my body to wait as I continue licking Lara's clit. Her wet hair surrounding my face is so erotic and human. When she finally reaches her climax, I hold her to me until every aftershock has been reached.

l. Many males have made me orgasm. However, they all had tentacles and would use their suckers to stimulate my clit. Although it was satisfying it felt like an itch being scratched. I felt nothing emotionally. Gael's gentle tongue between my legs was blunter but more sublime and for the first time in my life, it mattered that a certain person was giving me pleasure. And the way he's holding me now, for the small contractions following climax and rubbing my backside leads me to believe he enjoyed it too. I watch as he stands, his ridged organ wet at the tip. I want to lick it, but when I try to get to my knees, he stops me. And then before I can say anything, his hands are underneath my arms and he's hoisting me up. I instinctually wrap my legs around his trim waist, and he moves his hips to position himself at my core's entrance. I've never wanted to impale myself on anyone before. But now I want gravity to slide me down and my wet entrance to cover his hard ridged cock. I look into his green eyes and will him to do it. "Enter me, Gael. I want to feel what it's like to have a man."

g. I can feel her desire dripping out of her vagina and I hope that I can last more than two strokes. I hold her tight as I slowly move her small body down. Her wet, hot sex is enveloping me, and I close my eyes against everything else in the galaxy. All I can concentrate on is the up and down of her tightness. Somewhere in the back of my mind, I think about how small tentacles can be. And that my penis may be the largest thing that has ever entered her. It's a terrible thought that I'm even more aroused by this. I move her body faster and faster on top of me. I can feel the sway of her breasts against my chest, and I think I'm in heaven. I kiss her mouth passionately, my tongue finding hers, seeking out my orgasm which I thought would come immediately but instead has turned into a long, drawn out, intense affair in this dirty room on the edge of the galaxy.

l. I have never had a man's organ inside of me before. It feels so different and the way his body fits with mine. This. This is what sex is supposed to feel like. I want this to last forever. The way he picks me up like I weigh nothing and moves me to fit into him so perfectly. There's nothing but pure and natural desire here and I want this forever. I want to tell him, but I don't want to disrupt his rhythm.

g. My arms are numb from holding her, but I don't stop. I'm so close to coming now. Faster and faster I plunge her up and down impaling her on me. Her breasts are bouncing against my chest wildly driving me even harder. I can't hear or see anything. It's only her body taking me. I groan as I come into her. Hot semen shooting up her small human body. Once I've regained myself, shakily I put Lara on her feet, but I don't let go until I'm sure she's stable.

l. I feel his hot liquid running down my thighs. I reach down and touch it. Then I make eye contact with Gael. I don't know what I'm supposed to do. Is it rude to flick it off? Or is it unclean to let it continue to run down my legs?

g. Lara looks up at me, her lips swollen from my kisses and her pale cheeks red from physical exertion. She holds up her fingers with my come on them. I bring her fingers into her mouth. It's so sexy to watch her suck her fingers with my semen on it. When she's finished, I bring her fingers down again between her legs. There's so much come there. I scoop the liquid up with her fingers and bring them back to her mouth where I watch her lick it off. This time she uses her tongue expertly in a swirl. *Where was that tongue action when we were kissing?*

l. Now that I know he wants me to swallow all his semen, I use my skills to please him. One thing I know how to do well is lick bodily fluids to please males. When I finish, he surprises me by kissing me again. I taste Gael, myself in his mouth, and his semen all swirling together. I put my arms around his shoulders and again, I want him to enter me. But after a minute he lets go.

g. "I almost forgot where we are and what we are doing," I say and hand her her clothing. Then I put on my own quickly and get my gun.

l. "What's the rush?"

Chapter 7

Gael

"We still have some business to take care of," I tell her. I don't want to tell her what I'm planning on doing because it needs to be done no matter what. Once she is dressed, I lead her back out into the main temple. The abbess and an Agnorrian nun are there. I look around and the temple is mostly deserted. "It's done."

"You may leave," says the abbess. "You have satisfied the Goddess of Fertility."

"Just one more thing, you must not register that we are married."

"No."

I put Lara behind me with one hand and put a gun to the abbess's head.

Her yellow eyes look up at me not surprised. "I expected this, Imperial pirate."

And then I notice the Agnorrian has a gun on Lara.

"You can't hold a gun on two people at the same time," says the abbess. "Now you have a choice, you walk out of here with your human, or we kill her. Either way I win."

I continue to hold my gun against the abbess's head. "And I kill you too."

She smiles. "Do it."

I look into her yellow eyes and make a decision. I pull the trigger and shoot the Agnorrian nun before she can shoot Lara. I win. The Agnorrian falls to the floor in a puddle of purple blood. The abbess tries to knock the gun out of my hand, but I grab one of her tentacles so roughly it'll break off if I begin shaking her. "You can die too, or you can forget to report Lara's marriage. It's your choice."

"What makes you think I'll keep my promise?"

"Because if you don't, I've friends who enjoy torturing females and I've no doubt torturing an abbess would be the highlight of their year. So, it's up to you really."

"Fine." She spits on my face.

I wipe it off. "No need for goodbye kisses." I pick up Lara and walk out of the temple. I don't want her walking anymore on her bloody feet. As I place her in my transport, I look at her dirty and bloody body. I see some red between her legs. "Did I hurt you?"

She squeezes her legs together to hide the dried blood. "It felt good."

I meet her green eyes. She's lying. I'll have to deal with this later, we don't have time now.

Chapter 8

Gael and Lara

{Duet}

l. “Do you kill a lot of innocent people?” Ten minutes ago, I thought Gael was the most wonderful man ever, but then directly after being so tender with me, he kills an innocent nun. Not that I hadn’t seen cold-blooded murder before, just never from someone I thought I liked. My ears and heart are still ringing from the last hour.

g. “She wasn’t innocent. They were both standing in the way of us leaving safely.”

l. “How do you mean? The abbess said she was going to let us go if we married and we married.”

g. “As I said, everything there is streamed across the galaxy for those that are interested. And a human and Imperial will draw an audience. Those are exactly the people we’re out to fool. If she’d reported that we’d married on top of having sex, then there’d be no way that you could help me save trafficked humans.”

l. “Why?”

g. “Because I need you to be sold as a pet. And to do that you can’t be reported as being married to me. This way people will think I went to the temple to have sex with you, then stole you away and granted you freedom. I couldn't do anything about the live feed, but I could control the news of our marriage."

l. "What does legality even matter now? No one really thinks humans are free."

g. "You'll see in time."

l. His answer frustrates me. "Do you think anyone will be so foolish to believe that I'd give up my freedom to go back into slavery?"

g. "Many Imperials think that humans want to be owned. It wouldn't be difficult for any of them to believe that after being set free you decided you preferred captivity and allowed yourself to be caught. Don't give me that look. At the temple you said 'yes' to leaving with me no matter what I asked and that included being a pet. *You* were the one who proposed marriage."

l. "I didn't realize freedom was on the table." Then I ask before I think about it too much and lose my courage, "Are we really married?"

g. She asks about our marriage so innocently it almost takes my breath away. I look over at her. So small and almost naked in the navigator's chair. "Yes, it's legal."

l. "I thought if I ever married it would be different." I didn't mention that I got this idea from books from Earth. I'm sure he'd think I was a fool for being so naïve.

g. "I'm sorry I disappointed you. I did the best I could. At least I didn't lie you down on that filthy floor..."

l. I cut him off, "No, I mean, I thought everything would be different. More words and less murder." Then a thought occurs to me, "Have you been married before? Is this something you do often?" He could have a hundred wives for as casually as he's acting about the whole thing.

g. I open my mouth then close it. I count to seven in my mind and then say evenly, “No. I never thought about marrying anyone. And no, I’ve never married before nor will I ever marry again.”

l. I can tell I’ve made him annoyed with my questions. I don’t want him to kill me. I want my freedom, so I change the subject. “Is there a particular person you want me to be sold to?” I ask wondering if everything I felt for him was my fantasy only.

g. “Kamos.”

l. “You mean Kamos *Kamos*? The Kamos who is the kingpin for all illegal activity in the Imperial side of the galaxy and who recently publicly tortured and executed twenty Dulu for not fulfilling his order and the IGC did nothing about it?”

g. “Yes. I want you to infiltrate his palace and steal a teleportation suit.”

l. “How will I do that?”

g. “Allow yourself to be sold at Gala and charm him as his human pet.”

l. “No. I’m not doing Gala again. Ask anything else and I’ll do it for my freedom. But not that.”

g. “It’s the only way.”

l. “There must be another way.”

g. “Kamos only buys his human pets from Gala. He only trusts one specific trader and that’s because that trader never does private deals on the side or takes bribes. Everything is always business in the open with pets’ provenances.”

l. “Slavery isn’t a just business.”

g. “I didn’t say it was *just*. I said it was ‘business.’ Lara, please. Think of the other humans at Gala right now, as long as the IGC refuses to uphold the law and allow people to use loopholes, humans will never truly be free. So we must use whatever means necessary to return them to Earth while the law about returning, which *is* enforced, still allows."

l. "I *am* thinking about them. I can't get the memories out of my mind because *I* was one of them."

"Docking," a computerized voice says.

g. "What else are you going to do? Live out the rest of your days at the Fertility Temple until an Agnorrian picks you and you die from his poisonous penis sending toxins through your body over two days which I'm sure the abbess would film every gruesome moment of and sell for a tidy sum? Is that what you want as your legacy?"

l. "I'm human. I don't have a legacy."

g. "I'm giving you an opportunity to make one. If not for you, for others who want to be free."

l. I slap him out of frustration. "I want to be free." I look at my hand. It stings. I've never slapped anyone before. But I don't take back my action. More than anything I want to be free, but I still remember the horrors of Gala.

g. I'm glad she hit me, but I won't frustrate her more by smiling. *She'll do perfectly for this mission.* "Here we are. My ship the *Sisu.*"

l. I scrutinize the large ship as we dock. I see numerous guns on its port side. "Is that an Imperial word?"

g. "No, it's from Earth. It means 'grit.'"

l. "Why not just call your ship *Grit*?"

g. "Because 'sisu' means more and sounds better. It's Finnish. Look it up in the database and the history of those people. Humanity needs sisu if we are ever going to survive as equals in the galaxy."

l. "You're only half human," I point out. Immediately I wish I could take the words back when I see the look on his face. But the emotions

I saw are gone in a flash.

g. "That's true. But given how I was brought into the galaxy, I don't recognize my Imperial heritage as legitimate. And even if that weren't the case, I'm a moral man. Slavery is wrong and I've made it my life's work to stop it."

l. "The laws have already been changed," I say even though I know this is ridiculous. "But, those laws haven't done me any favors."

g. "They have and you've already benefitted from them."

l. "How? I haven't. I should've been granted freedom when Lord Juo died according to the new laws."

g. "The new laws allowed you to propose marriage to me. And now you have a husband."

l. I want to ask him again if we are *really* married, and what that entails, because his answer before was ambiguous. But the transport doors are opening and fierce-looking Imperial people are waiting to talk to him, no doubt some of his crew.

Chapter 9

Gael

We land and are met by my first officer and doctor. Both, like me, look Imperial with grey skin and black hair.

"This is my first officer, Seo, and my doctor, Hela."

"I don't speak Imperial," she says.

"But your translator."

Lara gives me the galactic sign for 'absolutely not' by crossing her forearms and then explains, "My master always had a fear that I'd join an Imperial cult and run away. As I said before, you're the first Imperial I've ever met."

We all stare at her for a minute. Agnorrian is the lingua franca on the side of the galaxy, but on the side we're returning to, it's Imperial. It's shocking to hear her translator is blocked against the Imperial language. Clearly her master was racist. *He probably had a secret Imperial pet.* I meet Seo's eyes, we're thinking the same thing. Then I explain to Lara, "I'm the only one who speaks English here. Please go with my doctor, her name is Hela. She can understand you, but you won't be able to understand her. She only speaks Imperial. Perhaps your translator can be modified."

Lara looks like she's going to say something and then decides against it.

I watch as Lara follows Hela from the docking bay. Then I turn to Seo, "She's reluctantly agreed. She had a horrendous time at Gala before, that's what's holding her back. Set in a course for the rendezvous. We can't be caught bringing her in. The false narrative must look accurate, that she escaped with me and then later turned herself over to be sold because she wants to be owned."

"Understood. Also, I just want to let you know, some of us here watched you and Lara just to make sure you weren't double-crossed at the Fertility Temple."

"I would've expected nothing less. I hope that we put on a good show."

"Superb. She's something..."

I cut him off right there. "I never want you to talk about what you saw between us or what sexual fantasies you might have about Lara. Not with me or anyone else. And tell the crew. Lara is one of us now and I want her treated with the same dignity and respect."

"Yes. I understand."

I've stunned Seo, but I would have said this for any person joining the crew. We've all done things we wished we wouldn't have had to in our lives. We shouldn't be held accountable for every action as if circumstances in life are always the same. "I'm going to shower. I'll meet you on the bridge in 30 minutes."

Chapter 10

Lara

I assume Gael has a lot to do and will meet me later to discuss his plan. So, I follow the tall Imperial woman with short black hair from the docking bay and through the hallways of the ship. It's busy with grey Imperials everywhere.

"Where are all the humans? Oh, I forgot you don't speak English."

She pulls out an IC and says through the handheld translator, "Safe."

I'm not impressed with that answer. "Safe on Earth or safe in eternal sleep?"

"Mostly safe on Earth."

"I heard Gael kills those he can't save."

"Sometimes. He does what's best, but he always gives people a choice. If given the opportunity, would you have rather had death than the life you had with your Uru master?"

"I would've rather had freedom."

"Obviously, but freedom usually isn't an option."

As we enter a decent looking medical center, I'm guided over to an exam station. "You can bathe and rest after my exam."

The doctor begins her assessment of me and a young man, probably her assistant, joins us. She begins speaking in Imperial to him. I only pick up that it's a tonal language. I can hear five maybe six tones.

Suddenly the doctor says through her translator, "I will have to study your translator. It's not designed in the usual way. Or I could try downloading Imperial onto it and see what happens?"

"What's the worst that could happen?"

"Brain damage."

"I'll wait."

"Good choice."

The doctor continues her ministrations quietly speaking in Imperial to the young man who's either taking notes or handing her medical instruments. She asks me about my head injuries, and I tell her about the sadistic nun.

"You're lucky you were able to leave," she says through the translator. "It must have been quite horrific for you to have gone from a protected life with Lord Juo to the Fertility Goddess's Temple. We currently don't have a counselor onboard, but I'd recommend you speak to one and consider having that time erased from your memory."

"I'm fine now," I say but the doctor doesn't seem convinced, but I can see on her face that she isn't going to contradict me.

"Please follow Sem, he's going to show you to your quarters. It's not much, but you can bathe, rest and put on some clean clothing."

I get up and follow the young man through more hallways, but these are less crowded. Then he opens a door for me. Inside is a single bed, a little window and what looks like a bathroom. I go in and he follows me and opens the little closet.

"You can wear these," he says in heavily accented English. Seeing my surprised face he explains, "My mother was human. Most of us on this ship," he swirls one of his grey hands around, "are half human or a quarter human."

I nod, not really knowing what to say with this information. I feel overwhelmed. I've only seen Agnorrians in passing who have a humanoid shape for the last 15 years and now I'm surrounded by grey skinned humans and it's kind of making me feel like I'm in a strange dream.

The young man reciprocates my nod and then quietly leaves.

I check the door after he's left. It's unlocked. I open and close it many times to make sure I'm not hallucinating. I even walk out into the hallway a few times and then walk back in.

Am I really free to move in and out of my room?

Well, as free as it is to be signed up with vigilante freedom fighters and married. Although I don't know how real my marriage is and I may have to relive my worst hell soon and die, but for the moment I am free to open and close my own door which exhilarates me.

After I'm satisfied with the door situation I return to my small quarters and go into the bathroom. It's nothing like the luxury I'm accustomed to when I was in my cage in the menagerie, but compared to the Fertility Temple, it's magnificent. I strip off the remnants of my gold clothing and turn on the water. When the temperature is right, I stand under it and watch as my gold coloring intermixed with blood and filth washes away down my legs, onto my feet, and away. I feel some sadness as I watch the gold-colored water turn clear.

Once I've washed myself with the simple soap I dry off and look for some kind of lotion for my skin. I find none, only a comb for my hair. I use it trying not to snap my hair that's now knotted from the soap.

When I'm satisfied that I could do the best I could, I find the clothing the young man Sem pointed out to me and put it on. It's large on my frame and the fabric is coarse, but I tell myself that this is what freedom feels like and a human like me should expect no more.

I get into the small bed then which also has rough blankets and put my whole head underneath the covers because I'm cold. I realize the lights are still on but I'm too tired to get up and figure out how to turn them off, so I just look at my dim little cave under the blankets and think about Gael and everything that's happened today. And I do my best to ignore thinking about the future.

I just want to live in this moment. Gael the Returner saved me. Just like from my childhood dreams. Except in those dreams not only did he marry me but we moved back to Earth and lived in a house like The Brady Bunch House.

He did marry me for whatever that is worth. But being here in this room doesn't signal to me he sees it as real.

I wake up with a start. I don't remember where I am, at first. I look around at the unfamiliar room and try to place it. After a second, I relax. I remember. I'm on Gael's ship.

I get up and can't resist opening my door. Again, I'm amazed it just opens and closes for me. No locks. No guards.

I've no idea what time it is, but it can't be too early as I see a few people in the hallway as I play with my door. People stop and stare, but I just stare back at them. And then they stare back then they leave.

When a third person doesn't walk away, I say, "What are you looking at? Humans opening and closing doors must be a common pastime on a ship that rescues humans from captivity."

The young woman just gives me a look of sympathy and then finally walks away.

I know I should feel ridiculous from the pleasure I get from opening and closing my door, but it feels so good, I just can't stop to care about what anyone else thinks of me right now.

"I heard you were playing with your door," I hear the doctor say through a translator from behind me.

"Good morning, Hela. Have you been sent to check on my mental state?"

"No. I know you're in your right mind. And it seems perfectly reasonable to me you take some pleasure in this."

"Have you figured out my translator issue?"

"Yes and no. As far as I can see your Uru master made it impossible to change or remove your translator without causing you brain damage. It seems he was a very jealous master indeed. There does seem to be a release code but I've no idea how to go about finding it given that his belongings were ransacked and stolen."

"I can't say I'm surprised about my translator. He was a decent master, but he was ruthlessly protective of his property."

"This being the case you'll have to learn Imperial the old-fashioned way. Your tutor will meet you in an hour. Given the number of languages you already speak it should go rather quickly."

I meet her eyes. "How much time do I have?"

"A little longer than a month, I imagine. You must learn enough to work the locks in Kamos's palace."

"I don't know if I can do that." Suddenly the simple enjoyment of opening and closing my door is gone.

"You must. Sooner or later the nuns at the Fertility Temple are going to report you as married. You must be sold before that information becomes public."

"So, you think it's better Kamos buys me and then finds out I'm a spy while I'm helpless in his lair?"

"No, he'll be so charmed by your beauty that he won't believe the rumors. No offense but you don't look dangerous."

I smile. "I don't know if that's a compliment or not given the situation. But I'll need better clothing if you expect me to seduce him into buying me. I can't do it wearing this."

"That's been taken care of. You need to meet Gael in his quarters. He has clothing for you."

"Where are his quarters?" I try to keep the disappointment out of my voice that he sent me to be alone after we married.

Hela points to a section on the wall of the ship and it lights up. Then she says something in Imperial I can't understand. With the translator she says, "Follow the green circle. It will lead you to his quarters."

Hela walks away and I do as she says. I walk for about five minutes until the circle stops moving forward. I assume I have arrived but there are two doors here. I can't read the Imperial writing on either of them. As I begin to say, "Eeny meeny miny moe," Gael opens the door and I almost fall backwards. He looks better than he did yesterday, well rested and smells delicious. My stomach begins to flip and it's not because I haven't eaten.

Chapter 11

Gael and Lara

{Duet}

l. "I didn't know which door."

g. "I see. Come in. We have a lot to talk about." I lead her into my quarters and present her with an array of sexy clothing we have onboard just for this purpose. "Do you think any of this will work?"

l. I pick up some of the pieces of fabric and rub it between my thumb and forefinger to get a sense of its quality. "It's not ideal but it might do the job. But to be honest I don't know what Imperial men like." I look through the pile for something silver or gold. "I'll also need gold paint and jewelry. The IGC took everything when they processed me."

g. "Gold paint isn't a problem, but we don't have any gold jewelry." I cross the room and open my own private collection. I pull out a silver ring with a small purple stone in it. "But I think this would work well and it's got an old tracking device on it. One that won't be noticed."

l. I take the small ring and turn it in my fingers. It's a minimal design, but has beauty. "This has a tracking device? Why? Is it made for spies?"

g. "Not at all. It's an Imperial lovers' ring. They're an ancient tradition. Lovers wear them to prove that they have nothing to hide."

l. I try the ring on my ring finger and show my hand to Gael theatrically. "Why do you have a lovers' ring?"

g. "It was my mother's."

l. I try to hand the ring back.

g. "I have no reason to keep it in a box. This seems like the perfect opportunity to use it and it might bring you luck. My mother would have fully approved of this plan."

l. I turn over the ring in my hand. "I don't want to lose it."

g. "Then don't lose it."

l. "Will you wear the matching one? Did your father give it you?"

g. "I'll wear the other one, but my father didn't give it to me."

l. Before I can ask him about this admission, he holds up one of his grey hands.

g. "I don't discuss my family."

l. "I understand. Neither do I," I say. I wouldn't be surprised if this was a rule among his crew. *Who wants to talk about their personal sorrows in the galaxy?* It's better to just move on and take every day as it comes.

g. "Hela told you about the translator issue?"

l. "Yes, but I don't know how quickly I can learn Imperial."

g. "Learn as much as you can as quickly as you can. When you arrive in Kamos's palace there'll be other humans who'll be fluent and can continue to teach you. But remember trust no one."

l. "What is the plan then? I thought I was there to liberate the other humans?"

g. "Only after you return here with the teleportation suit."

l. "But..."

g. "Do you know what Stockholm Syndrome is?"

l. "No."

g. "It's when you fall in love with your captor."

l. "Who'd do that?"

g. "Oh, you'd be surprised. Many people. It's easier than accepting reality."

l. I begin to question this, but he cuts me off.

g. "There's not enough time to talk about it now, but trust me, I've been doing this for long enough to know that not everyone is thrilled to be liberated. The plan is this; you get in there, gain enough trust that you can find out where the teleportation suit is and then use it to escape. I'll be at a nearby rendezvous point so you don't have to go far. And with this ring at that distance, you'll be able to contact me so that I know when you're escaping."

l. "There's another issue. Besides the fact that I don't speak or read Imperial. I also have never teleported or operated a teleportation device let alone a military prototype."

g. "It won't be difficult to understand. I'll have your language tutor run you through how teleportation works. My main concern is you getting through Gala."

l. "Me too."

g. "Hela says that she can give you some calming drugs before you enter."

l. "I don't want to be drugged out. What if I have to fight? I need something that'll make me feel invincible."

g. "There's a black market drug that does that, but I don't know how long it lasts."

l. "I want it."

g. "Did you have to fight last time?"

l. "Yes. I was pitted against another young girl and we had to fight to the death for spectators. It was horrible."

g. "I'm sorry you have to go back, but it's for a greater purpose. Imagine if you could've been saved and sent back to Earth when you were eight years old."

l. I'm not crying but tears are running down my cheeks thinking about that little girl I was then. I would do anything to save her right now. I can still see her crying in Gala. Scared, hungry, and angry.

g. I bring up images of the humans that have just been brought into Gala. "You can save most of these girls, Lara. Get me that suit from Kamos."

l. "I wish I could go back in time and save myself," I whisper. I'm not even trying to hold back the tears now thinking of myself as a young girl. I had forbidden myself from remembering all of this before. But now it seems like I've no self-control and my mind is forcing me to remember.

g. I put a comforting hand on Lara's petite shoulder. "If I ever get my hands on a time machine..."

l. I smile up at him. "Just give humans all the technology they need to rule the galaxy so no one decides it's a great idea to start abducting us."

g. "It wouldn't even take that. All that needs to change is Earth joining the IGC when they were first asked during Earth's mid-twentieth century."

l. "You really think that would've made such a difference?"

g. "Yes. Imperials have a strange closeness with humans. And I believe humanity could've also influenced the Empire for the better.

Maybe in a different timeline that happened. Just remember no matter how similar Imperials feel to you, they can be just as ruthless as any other species in the galaxy."

l. "Please don't underestimate me, I've been among aliens most of my life. I know what it means to be human in the galaxy. People assume I'm hardly sentient with a short memory and only basic emotions."

g. "Good. The last woman who infiltrated Kamos's palace stayed. Rumor has it she fell in love with him."

l. "How many women have you sent on this mission before me?"

g. "Only two. The first was killed. We were told it was over a dispute not related to the mission, but that's second-hand information."

l. "How was she killed?"

g. "It was alleged that she was strangled."

l. "And you don't think Kamos suspects Terra Ka is feeding him women?"

g. "Of course, he suspects which is why he only uses one trader on Gala and that trader has a connection of trusted traders *he* only uses. But you see if you dig deep enough there's always a chink in the armor, you can always find someone who's having a bad day and is blaming someone else up the food chain. And so we use those unhappy traders."

l. "And you don't think I'm going to be obvious given it's no secret where I just came from?"

g. "It's true, it might be obvious, but you're probably the last chance we'll have to try this particular plan. And I've high hopes for you, Lara. Unlike the other women, I think you know what's going to be expected of you and you can do the job without being too affected by...."

l. "The sex," I fill in for him.

g. "I reckon you've been educated in these matters. Not the penetration part, but the rest." I search her green eyes to gauge how she's feeling. The last thing I want to do is to send her to Kamos knowing what happens with human pets there.

l. "Does it make you uncomfortable to talk about it even after what we did? Have you had your fill of me sexually and now you're ready to pass me off for another's use?" That's what all males seemed to do to me. They would touch me and then be done with me. No one ever came back.

g. Her words cut me, but I use all my self-control to remain calm. "As I first mentioned at the Fertility Temple, I didn't want to have sex with you. But," I say quickly noting her lowered face expression, "that doesn't mean I didn't enjoy what we did together nor do I deny our marriage. But in this instance, when talking about your suitability for this mission, I'd be just as uncomfortable to talk to someone who is about to be tortured for me." Since I met this woman, I've had a stone in my stomach thinking about sending her to Kamos. Especially now that she's my wife. *Am I insane to send her?* "I'm asking you to do something you don't want to do. Don't assume for a second that I take that lightly or that I think you'll enjoy being an Imperial man's pet."

l. "Many people would. They believe I like it. I've been forced to endure sexual abuse from unwanted males because the alternatives were always worse. But no one wants to admit, 'I had no choice.' Because if they did, then they'd be admitting their society isn't perfect and they turned a blind eye to my suffering."

g. "And many people are fools which is why this plan may *actually* work. You know exactly how to play this part. You know that people who own pets, no matter how much they adore their pets, those pets will never be seen as equal."

l. "I think you might be a fool too. I'm the third woman you are sending. Are you sure you're not a fool?" Gael smiles at me for the first time and I'm struck by his sincerity.

g. "Lara, you can be the judge of that. Take the ring and the clothing. I'll arrange some gold paint. Your language lesson starts soon in the conference room."

l. "I don't know how to get there."

g. "Down the hall and on the right. I'll escort you."

l. We reach the conference room and it's empty. "Has my language teacher not arrived?"

g. I greet her formally in Imperial and bow. "I am your language teacher."

l. He has a glint in his eye that makes me smile. "You could have said so."

g. "I like to compartmentalize things. Maybe too much. Anyway, I am the only one who is fluent in English and Imperial. Please sit down. We have a lot to cover."

l. Gael sits across from me at the table and says something in Imperial. I repeat his words. They sound wrong and feel unfamiliar in my mouth. "Did you teach the other women who were sold to Kamos?"

g. "No. They had translators."

l. "I heard that was illegal to give a human a translator in the Empire. It was one of the reasons my master hated Imperials."

g. I shrug. "As everything in the galaxy it's a grey area. There are still human pet experts who say that if you give a human a translator they'll get brain damage. It doesn't matter that it's not true, people want it to be true because it's much easier to keep a pet that can't fluently talk to you. Now, Kamos will know your background with Lord Juo which will make you very attractive to him and you'll be even more attractive if you speak some Imperial."

l. "I don't know how much I can learn in a month."

g. "You speak Agnorrian. It's one of the most difficult languages in the galaxy."

l. "I was surrounded by Agnorrians and Uru. I didn't have a choice."

g. "But you still maintained your human language even after puberty despite being the only human."

l. "My master imported entertainment from Earth to keep me occupied when I was alone. I also had an AI to *talk* to, but that pretty much just always told me what I wanted to hear. Lord Juo would have it rebooted every so often because it began coming up with scenarios of how I could escape. One of its solutions was suicide. Lord Juo wanted the 'perfect human specimen' and he couldn't have that if I was thinking about death."

g. "That must have been very lonely," I say imagining being stuck in a cage and the only physical contact she had was with tentacled aliens touching her erotically. I reach out my hand to cover hers. "You're here with us now. Humans and Imperials are the same. We have the same DNA and after you return from Kamos, I swear you'll never be locked in a cage as the perfect human specimen ever again."

l. "I don't like being called that."

g. "Good. You shouldn't. And remind yourself of that when you feel like you can't learn Imperial. That's what Imperials like to believe that humans are too stupid to speak their language. That's what makes them different from Agnorrians or the Uru. Imperials know humans are genetically the same but use their high position in the galaxy to exploit humans for their own pleasure and economic gain. With every Imperial word you learn you are taking away some of their power. Now are you ready to begin?"

l. "I'm ready to be liberated. Give me the keys to do it." I feel the ancient lovers' ring heat up and I look at Gael for an explanation. He's wearing the matching one.

g. "When we are both happy or determined and close by they become warm. That's how you'll be able to signal me when the time comes, through your emotions. I can feel your emotions and you mine. If we feel the same they become very warm like they are now. But if we heighten them even more over a period of say, at the 15th hour, on the 5th day of the week that can be our signal."

l. "Why would anyone create rings that do that?" I ask, looking at the ring as if it's going to do something else. I've only ever heard of tech jewelry but never worn any.

g. "As a reminder to think about the other person."

l. I stop myself from saying, 'And your parents wore these even though she was a pet?' Obviously, it was a very complicated relationship for him. Instead, I say, "Thank you for taking the time to teach me." He puts his other large grey hand across the table. Now he's holding both of my hands. His green eyes meet mine. And I feel like I can't breathe. Images from yesterday pass through my mind, him with his head between my legs and I can feel my body become aroused for him. I'm sure he must feel the same because our rings become frighteningly hot. I want him to enter me again with his ridged phallus, lick my clit, and whisper in my ear.

g. I can smell her fresh desire and see it reflected in her eyes. More than anything I want to throw her across this table and ravage her petite human body. But how can I do that knowing what I know about her past and her future? I don't want her to ever think of me as a man who took advantage of her for sex. I'm her husband after all. I force myself to think of the most unsexy thing I possibly can and say sincerely, "You are risking everything for me and Terra Ka. It's a privilege to teach you what I can." I hold her gaze hoping that these won't be the only days I know Lara, my human wife. "Now let's begin, repeat after me..."

Chapter 12

Lara

I fall down on my bed not bothering to take off my clothing. It's so late. I'm exhausted. Imperial is a sophisticated language with complex grammar and the possibility for compound word combinations is endless. And Gael is a demanding teacher. I can still hear his voice ringing in my ears, 'That's the wrong tone. You've just said you sing like an eggplant. Do it again.'

As I drift off into that strange place between conscious and subconscious Gael is there waiting for me. I tell him I'm too tired to practice anymore and that all the tones are muddled in my head. But then he extends his hand to me and tells me we're going to practice something else entirely.

I've spent my life hiding my emotions, so I hide them now. I don't want to let Gael know how attractive I find him. Every part of him. And how much I wish our marriage was real but in the last few weeks, he's made no effort to show any romantic affection towards me. The only thing I have now is my memory of us at the Fertility Temple and my dreams. I take his hand and he leads me to a bedroom. A nondescript dream bedroom.

"I want to seduce you," he says in the dream.

I don't trust myself to respond so I say nothing. But I want him. I've endured males my whole life, but Gael has awakened something inside of me that I never knew existed. I never understood why any woman would willingly chase a man. But now. *Now I know.* I want Gael so much and I want all of him, not just the sex. I think this is love. I've never loved anyone but the more time I spend with Gael, the more he teaches me about Terra Ka and the Imperial language, the more I want to be with him.

Gael begins touching me with his large hands and then suddenly... my alarm is going off.

I open my eyes. My hands are between my legs, my thighs are wet, and my lights are all on. It's morning.

"Well, this isn't impressive," I say to myself. I never used to have dreams like this, but now it's almost every night. I get out of bed and go to the toilet. Then I take a quick shower. I don't want to smell like I've been touching myself, not that I have much of a reputation to uphold since I was kept as property and then rescued from the sex temple, but I don't need to give anyone anymore reminders of what I've done.

Once I'm dressed, I hurry to breakfast. Gael doesn't keep strict Imperial hours on his ship, but he does like everyone to eat breakfast at roughly the same time. He says it makes for a more harmonious crew.

I run into the dining hall and quickly take some food from the buffet, plain porridge and tea. Breakfast isn't over yet but I was one of the last to come in. The others look up at me and those close to me greet me with the standard morning greeting which I can now reply with my basic Imperial. I feel everyone on this ship looks at me with mixed emotions. Sometimes pity and other times curiosity. And I feel the same way towards them. How strange that one of their parents was human and was kept like a pet? And how they now have dedicated their lives to saving humans, but when they look in the mirror, they only see grey Imperial faces.

I briefly breached the subject with Gael but he said his appearance was a reminder of everything that could go wrong in the galaxy which didn't make sense to me, but he told me there wasn't any time to talk about it. He says that about a lot of things, and I always let it go. What do I really know about the galaxy? I've only watched it from a safe distance.

But looking at the crew of the *Sisu* I can't help but wonder what I would do with a half Imperial child if I became pregnant. Lord Juo made sure all my admirers were vetted and it was next to impossible any of them could impregnate me anyway, but I doubt Kamos will be so careful. In fact, he may want his pets to breed.

If it happened to me, what would I do? Would I keep the half Imperial child or give it away? Would I even have a choice?

Gael reckons it'll take me a few months to accomplish my goal, but I know more about seducing men and fooling women than he does. I think, at the earliest, I'll be able to accomplish this in a year.

I remind myself of the girls who've just been dropped at Gala. If I can get the device back in under a year, then Gael can initiate his most powerful plan yet to date, according to him. I, of course, don't know all what it'll entail, except his word that hundreds of humans will be saved. I have no reason not to believe him as he's renowned for repatriating humans.

My mind won't let it go though. He's also known for killing those he can't save.

Just then Gael enters the dining hall. We all look up as he's clearly not getting breakfast.

Chapter 13

Gael and Lara

{Duet}

g. "Everyone leave but Lara."

l. I'm glad my Imperial is good enough to understand what he's just said because his tone is commanding and is making my heartbeat faster. And this is an out of character interruption. I feel like I'm in trouble. I keep my face as neutral as possible as he watches me and everyone else quickly leaves their food behind and within seconds the dining hall is empty except for us.

g. I glance around to make sure everyone is gone before I approach Lara. "Are your nipples pierced?"

l. "Excuse me?"

g. "Are your nipples pierced?" I'm using Imperial because it sounds less invasive.

l. "I don't understand."

g. I repeat myself in English.

l. I reply in English, "No, they aren't."

g. "We must remedy that as soon as possible," I've switched back into Imperial.

l. "I can assure you my nipples are attractive just the way they are," I say as I cross my arms over my breasts protecting them from being pierced in the dining hall.

g. "This isn't about attractiveness. It's about leashes. All of Kamos women are led around by their nipples."

l. I hold my arms closer to my breasts thinking about my sensitive nipples.

g. "Most women, human pets or Imperial women, have this done soon after puberty. I just assumed since you were human that you also had this done. If we don't do it Kamos might find you less attractive at Gala. And if he buys you, he might take pleasure in doing it himself."

l. "Can I take the chance that he might like a woman without pierced nipples?"

g. "It's unlikely."

l. I meet Gael's green eyes. He looks at me like an equal. No man or woman has ever done that. I know he's honestly waiting for my opinion, but I don't know. "What would you do?"

g. "I'd pierce them here. I wouldn't want to make myself look difficult." I don't add that as her husband it would be my responsibility to do it. I don't want to be selfish. She's already doing enough by going to Kamos. I don't want to decide this for her too.

l. I consider his opinion and then make my decision. This is the first decision I've ever made about my body in my entire life. I don't want to share that with him explicitly, so I quietly pat myself on the back as I say, "Perhaps different won't be difficult in this instance. My provenance will be from Lord Juo. Market me as 'Fresh to the Imperial Market' without even my nipples pierced."

g. "That sounds terrible, but good, but terrible. I'm sorry..." I trail off. Can I really send Lara to do this? I'm unsure. I've fallen in love with her over these last weeks and every day she surprises me with her pragmatic courage. I've never met a woman like her and I'm afraid I'll never see her again.

l. I hold up my hand to stop Gael from feeling too guilty. "I'm choosing this. You freed me from the sex temple. This is my choice."

g. I look into Lara's green eyes and wonder what she's really thinking. She keeps herself locked up safe. It's for the better, I tell myself and then make the galactic sign for, 'it's settled then,' and walk out. On my way out I say in Imperial, "Lessons in five minutes in the conference room. Don't be late."

Chapter 14

Lara

"I can't believe I'm going to do this."

Hela looks up at me solemnly. "Think of the others you'll be saving." She takes my arm and inserts something under my skin. Then she takes my hand and runs it over where she's injected the drug. "Press here hard for three seconds when you want the drug. It should last you about six months if you don't use it more than once a day."

"How often can I use it?"

"You shouldn't use it at all if you can avoid it, but I'd say no more than twice a day."

"Any other side effects other than making me feel invincible?"

"As the drug wears off, after about an hour, you will experience depression, irritability, and possible excessive sweating. If you use this every day, you will become addicted to it and it can cause paranoia and anger."

"I understand."

"When you come back, I'll make sure we have a counselor onboard."

"I like your positive attitude." I want to tell her there's no reason for a counselor because I'm probably not coming back. The more I've studied about Kamos and learned about Imperial people, in comparison Gala seems like a decent place. Kamos rules his little corner of the galaxy with an iron fist.

Hela touches my shoulder and looks me in the eyes. "You will be successful."

In this moment, I actually do feel like I'll be able to do what they are asking of me, but I know that's only her telepathy convincing me of it. When it comes down to it, I'll have to overcome my fears of torture and death to succeed in this and I don't know if I'm strong enough. I've never been put to the test.

I leave the medical center and walk down to Gael's quarters. I know he's feeling nervous because my lovers' ring is slightly cold. Over these past several weeks, I've become accustomed to wearing it and as the ring promises, it makes you aware of the other person when they have extreme emotions. I have no idea how it works but I don't care to figure it out either.

As I'm walking down the hallway people gawk at me. I'm wearing my working clothes, if they can be called 'clothes.' A top made of rough gold fabric that barely covers my breasts and an even smaller gold covering for my sex. My backside is almost completely exposed. And I've covered myself in gold paint and brushed my hair all to one side as Agnorrian and Uru males find attractive. I've purposely done this to help my 'brand' as being sold as 'fresh' from the other side of the galaxy. I ignore the stares. *I'm working just as hard as everyone else.*

I arrive at Gael's door. When he lets me in, he's at his desk distracted. Then he looks up and I can't decipher the look that crosses his face.

Chapter 15

Gael and Lara

{Duet}

g. I knew what Lara would look like dressed as a gold human pet. I have revisited that memory of her in a shadow of this look when I first met her at the Fertility Goddess's Temple, but to see her now like this is completely different. I'm attracted to her appearance, now as I'm always attracted to her, but it's like she's a different person. It's not only her façade that's changed but she has a completely different demeanor. For the first time I feel less worried for her but at the same time remorseful that she must go. "You look different."

l. "I changed," I say softly. *What more can I say?* That I went from being his dutiful student to a vessel for alien men? I never want him to think of me as the latter, but how can he not? He knows exactly what I'll be doing. "It's all for the greater good."

g. "It is." I want to say something more than, 'thank you,' but I can't think. My mind is refusing to move forward with this farewell. I have sent many Terra Ka members into the field knowing I may never see them breathing again, but this is so different, and I can't stop my heart from beating so hard for her.

l. "What is sex anyway? Muscle contractions, a bit of bodily fluids. Women have made it so important because it's a way for the matriarchy to maintain its dominance. Insisting it's the ultimate pleasure to have sex with a woman," I say, trying to make this triter than it is. We both know the truth. Our rings are ice cold with regret for what never was, conversations we never had, and the truth that this might be the last time we ever see one another. I meet his green eyes. "Will you watch the auction?"

g. "Yes. Of course. Be safe and take this." I hand her a small vial.

l. "What's this? I can't read this word." I investigate the small vial and bring it up to my nose to smell it.

g. "Don't. It's poison. It'll look like you fell asleep, but you never wake up. It's for emergencies."

l. I try to hand it back. "I've been through worse. Someone will have to kill me. I won't do it myself."

g. "Keep it anyway. Maybe you'll meet someone else that needs it."

l. I want to give it back to him, but he just shakes his head. I put the small vial along the top seam of my golden bra. "Wish me luck."

g. "Thank you, Lara. Remember hundreds of humans are counting on you to set them free. Think of them when times are tough. Good luck. And remember the ring."

l. I subconsciously twist the lovers' ring on my finger when he mentions it. He's taught me everything about how to use it to contact him and the intervals he will be close enough to Kamos's palace for it to work. I only hope that it doesn't get taken away from me. But it's unlikely as it's not worth much and I'll be sold for a higher price if I look more expensive. I rise and put my hands on his black hair and kiss his forehead. "I will think of you when times are tough," I say in a whisper. And this is the truth. Last night when I couldn't sleep, I was thinking about my motivation for this mission. As much as I want to save those humans, especially the children, I recognized they're just numbers to me, nameless faces, and that they alone are not enough. But when I thought of Gael. My lovely Gael, I found the strength in myself to go today.

g. I'm spellbound by her actions. Is this part of her seduction trick? Is she already playing her role? Or does she expect me to say, 'Never mind we'll find someone else?' I don't know but I can't let her affect me anymore than she already does. This must be done and she's the most capable for the job. I take her hands in mine and stand. "As soon as you know where the teleportation suit is and think you might be able to escape contact me."

l. I'm struck by his lack of reciprocation about my honesty. But then again, he saves humans all the time. It's probably a common occurrence that a lot of the women he saves believes they're in love with him. It doesn't matter, I tell myself. I married him and I love him. I want to tell him even if my love is not requited. "Goodbye," I say in English and then turn and begin walking away. I walk slowly hoping he will say something.

g. My heart is going to beat out of my chest. It's so loud she must hear it too. Our lovers 'rings are so cold I'm sure there'll be a ring of frostbite on our fingers. I want to pull her back. I don't want to send her on this dangerous mission. There'll be someone else. I want Lara here with me. But I can't do that. I can't think of myself, then I'm just as terrible as my father. I must let her walk off this ship and do her duty for her fellow humans. "Good luck, Lara. My human wife. We will be waiting patiently for your signal."

Chapter 16

Lara

Sem pilots the transport to another waiting ship. As we're docking, he says to me in his accented English, "I don't believe in the goddesses, but I believe in a moral balance in the galaxy. For what you've suffered, the fates owe you this win. Remember that."

I put my hand on his arm. "Thank you."

He nods.

Once we are docked, I exit the transport, my bare feet cold against the hard floor. I have no time to take in my surroundings before I'm immediately put in chains.

Sem signs me over without even a glance in my direction.

I keep my eyes down. I need to play my part now.

I hear Sem say in Imperial, "She doesn't want to be free. Take her. I'd rather have the UCs than sex with a woman who's had Agnorrians and Uru tentacles all over her."

"You're sure?"

"Yes. I would rather have the UCs."

Sem receives the UCs and I watch his boots as he walks past me into the transport.

My chains are pulled and I'm led through this ship. Unlike the *Sisu*, this ship is heavily perfumed and the hallways are dimly lit. As we pass Imperials with black uniforms, I realize this is an Imperial military vessel. I begin to panic. I thought I'd be passed to a trader.

However, my fears dissipate when I'm shown to a small room with one bunk. My chain is connected to the bed. And I discover after my new captor has left the chain is just long enough for me to reach the toilet.

"Wakey wakey human."

It's completely dark. I'm exhausted. But then I remember where I am and what's going on. The chain around my wrist is yanked hard and I fall out of bed. Before I can tell my captor I have to use the toilet, he's pushing me towards it.

"We don't want you to have an accident while you're being sold."

I don't wait for privacy. I know what it means to be someone else's property. My body and my thoughts are not my own. I pull down my skimpy briefs and pee. Once I'm finished, I'm led through the hallways to a dining hall. I'm sat down and spoon-fed porridge. What surprises me is not that I'm being spoon-fed but that it's the same breakfast I had on Gael's ship. And the thought of him gives me courage.

After my temporary owner thinks I've had enough food and water, I'm escorted off the ship. I recognize the smell of Gala before we enter. It's a disgusting odor of death and the sweat of aliens intermixing in unthinkable ways. I gag for a second and my captor stops.

"Just let it sink in. I know it's a dreadful smell. You'll get used to it in a minute."

The last thing I want to do is let the smell of Gala sink in, but he's right. My nose and throat adjust after a minute. Then we continue walking.

Once we pass the threshold I hear the screaming, the auctioning, and the laughter. It's a horrible mix of sounds that probably only exist in alien slave markets.

As I'm led through on a chain, people start to look at me and holler. Some begin following us to the stall my new master is looking for. Thankfully my Imperial master is in a uniform and armed to the teeth so no one dares touch me. Once we reach the stall, there's quite a crowd of alien males surrounding us. All here for the show.

"I wondered when you would end up back in Gala, Lara. Pets like you can't survive on your own. You're what we call an 'indoor human.'"

I recognize the male selling me at Gala. It's the same Octopod who sold me the first time. But now he looks like he's been through some rough times and is missing a tentacle. *Good*, I think. Perhaps Sem is correct and there is some moral balance in the galaxy.

My Imperial captor and the Octopod trader come to an arrangement and my chain is passed to one of his tentacles. He pulls me close to him and once I'm close enough to smell his fishy breath he says, "You don't mind if I check if the goods are still as they should be?"

I don't say anything but turn my head away as his tentacles and suckers fondle my entire body. I send my mind elsewhere. I've been able to do it since I've been a girl. I see what's happening to me as if it's happening to another.

The Octopod trader's tentacles are inside my vagina, sucking on nipples through my top and another one in my mouth making me gag. All the while alien males look on, getting their UCs ready to purchase me.

When the Octopod removes his tentacles from my body he says, "Everything seems to be in order. You have to check with these Imperials." Then he calls over one of his assistants. "Put her in the cell. We will hold her back for the auction this evening."

At least I'll only have to be here a day, I tell myself. I'm led into a large cell with about 20 other human women and girls. I can tell by their clothing they've all been abducted from Earth recently. They all stare at me as I'm led in and then released from my chains.

Some of the women begin to cry when they see me. I understand. They know exactly what I'm used for. Others ask me if this is a movie set. If they're shooting some kind of pornography science fiction film because of my outfit. And the children desperately ask me if I'm a superhero. I don't know what to say besides, 'I'm no superhero.' Do I tell them it's as bad if not worse than they fear? Then I remember the poison. Should I discreetly offer it to them? Could I have a dead woman or worse a dead child on my conscience?

I take some water from a nearby communal jug and then sit down in the corner furthest away from the communal toilet.

A young woman comes to sit next to me. "How long have you been here?"

"Fifteen years." I look over at the children. "I was like them."

The young woman's brown eyes widen. "Do you have any advice?"

I shake my head. "It's all luck who buys you."

"But you've lasted for all these years, and you look healthy and not abused."

"I only look healthy on the outside. In my mind, I'm completely disfigured. I'm hardly human at all anymore." But as soon as I say this, I realize it isn't true. When I was with Gael and when he was kissing me, I was as human as I'd ever been. "Actually, I do have some advice, make yourselves as docile as possible and an Imperial will want you. It's your best chance of survival."

"Who are the Imperials?"

"The ones who look human but are grey."

"We've not seen any of them," another woman says from across the cell.

"They'll be here for the auction. And also know, it's illegal now to own humans."

Talking breaks out throughout the cell. "How are we here then?"

"Where are the alien police to stop this?"

"I know. It's complicated and illegal that we're all still here. But know that if you get a galactic citizen to set you free than you are free."

"How do we do that?"

"If I knew, I wouldn't be here," I say. Ironically, it's the truth. I don't even know if I was really free once I married Gael and the abbess let me go. I wish now I would've asked just so I could say to myself, 'I was free for a short time and I can be free again.'

"Anything else you don't know?" a teenager asks.

I look at her with pity. She's so young. "Don't let them break you. Learn to speak their languages and know that there's a resistance group called Terra Ka."

"Terra Ka what does that mean?"

"Earth Blue. They are vigilante justice seekers. They know you're here and will try to rescue you. Every human abducted has one galactic year during which they can be legally repatriated back to Earth. After that, you're stuck out here. I've heard that there are human traders who do make a living in the galaxy, but I've never seen any."

"You seem to know a lot for someone in the same circumstances as we are."

The young woman next to me defends me, "She's been here for 15 years and is still alive."

Then the whole cell goes quiet. I take the young woman's hand in mine and give her the small vial of poison. "If things get too tough, take this. You'll fall asleep and never wake up. There are some aliens that may buy you and a peaceful death would be better than what they would want from you."

She reluctantly takes the vial. "How will I know which are the bad ones?"

"Trust your instincts. We're human we can still recognize our predators by sight and smell."

I hear Kamos and his entourage arrive before I see them. There's chanting and shouting that becomes louder and louder as he gets closer. Our cell has no windows. It's not like the one below it which is all windows for display. I feel sorry for whoever is down there now. I know what they'll be forced to do unless this Octopod trader has changed his ways. Unlikely.

When Kamos has arrived at our stall the shouting becomes even louder as I assume the show below has begun.

"What's happening?" the young woman next to me asks in a frantic voice.

"A very powerful mafia Imperial called Kamos has come to buy some human pets."

The women around me start freaking out.

"Human pets?"

"What? We aren't pets!"

"You said this is illegal. How is this possible?"

"I want to wake up from this nightmare!"

The young woman next to me asks, "Is he one of the grey guys?"

"Yes."

"So I should try to go with him?"

At this point I wonder if I've made a mistake in telling them to be meek to attract Imperials. What if Kamos reaches his quota for humans with all of these women and doesn't take me? I decide in a split second that it's up to fate now anyway. "Yes. I'm going to try to go with him."

Our conversation is interrupted by more horrific screaming below.

"What's going on down there?"

I don't want to tell them. I stay quiet and put my hands over my ears. I try to drown out my own memory of what I did down there in that cell. But I will never forget the look on that other girl's face as I watched her life fade away.

After the shrieking has subsided and the cheering dies down, I hear our cell door being opened. A dozen or so males come in with chains and begin selecting which of us will be auctioned off.

A male stands in front of me and I stand when he motions the chain to go around my neck. Unlike the others, I have a gold chain and am led out first. My handler says to me as we go down the stairs, "You're to be auctioned first as it's your second time around at this stall. Think of it as a privilege."

I'm led through the doors to the auctioning stage and just as I remember it from before it's terrifying to be led out in front of hundreds of male aliens all looking at me as if I'm dinner. I want to press the medicine that Hela gave me, but I know that won't help me look like an attractive pet, so I resist.

I'm led up to a podium and my chain secured. I resist the urge to look out at the aliens. First because it might be too frightening and second because I might look suspicious if I don't look terrified.

The Octopod trader takes the floor next to my podium. "We all wondered what happened to Lara from Earth when Lord Juo died. Well look, here she is. She has returned from the other side of the galaxy. She speaks Agnorrian, Uru, Octopod, and a bit of Imperial. She's perfect for training. She's never been touched by a humanoid. Her nipples have never been pierced. Now should we start the bidding at one thousand UCs? Who wants to start with one thousand UC?"

I hear the bidding go up from the crowd. "One thousand five hundred UCs."

"Two thousand."

And then the chanting begins. "Show us the goods! Show us the goods!"

The Octopod trader stops the bidding and responds, "Come now she's almost naked as she is."

"Show us her nipples! Show us her nipples!"

I continue to look at my feet, but decide this will be a good time to press the medicine. I do it and over the next few seconds I begin to feel invincible. I can do this. I can seduce Kamos wherever he is out there and he'll never suspect I'm a spy.

I hear a defining voice say, "Five thousand UCs if she gives us a tantalizing show. I'm not buying defective used goods."

Everyone goes mad with delight. I assume this is Kamos himself to offer to pay so much if I perform.

My Octopod seller says to me, "Now Lara, if you would all entertain us?"

For the first time, I look up to my audience of alien males and begin to sing as I slowly begin to remove what little clothing I have. I can see I'm pleasing almost everyone, but Kamos is too far away for me to see his face expression. In fact, he's shrouded in shadow. I sing a sweet, slow, and seductive acapella. As I sing, I lightly run my hands over my arms and then circle my gold bra with my hands, tantalizingly playing with the straps. Then I run my hands over my legs beginning with my ankles and moving upwards, slowly, always slowly, making sure my fingers run over my sex to cause my underwear to get caught inside my folds. Next, I run my hands up my back, through my hair, and then down again. My hands go back to my shoulders and I pull my bra straps down one by one, before lifting my right breast out and displaying my unpierced nipple. I seductively put my fingers in my mouth when there's a break in the song and suck on them. I take them out of my mouth with a pop. I resume singing my sweet song as I run my wet fingers over my exposed nipple making it taut. The alien males go crazy for this. So I pull the other breast out from my bra and lick my fingers like a lollypop before caressing that nipple so that both are standing hard for all to see their natural perfection. I put my hands on my knees and bend over a little to make my breasts sway back and forth. The male aliens go wild, and some try to flick their tentacles up to catch my unpierced nipples but my Octopod trader swiftly swats their tentacles away. I smile and shake my finger at them like they are naughty schoolboys. Finally, I run my hands up my legs again, rubbing myself so that my underwear is stuck in me before slowly putting my hand down my underwear and touching my clit.

The alien males begin chanting again, "Show us your human fur! Show us your human fur!"

To oblige them, I turn around, bend over, and begin slowly peeling my underwear off. Then I turn around gracefully and rub my fingers through the blonde hair between my legs.

"Pleasure yourself! Pleasure yourself!"

I look over at my Octopod trader. He raises one of his tentacles for silence and then calls out to Kamos. "Lord Kamos, would you have her orgasm here in this public place for all of us?"

The chanting begins again while Kamos makes a decision.

I wait. I can do whatever is required of me. I'm a seductive genius. I press my arm again where Hela put the medicine and feel a new rush of confidence spread through my body.

"If she can make herself orgasm in one minute, I'll pay ten thousand for her. In two minutes, nine thousand and so forth. If it takes her more than ten minutes, you will give her to me for free. As a gift of a free show."

I know this isn't going to make the Octopod trader happy, but what can he do?

It takes him half a second to realize he has no options with me. "Accepted." Then he looks at me. "Orgasm fast."

Somewhere someone yells, "Prepare to start the timer!" and a large holographic timer appears. And it's counting down from ten minutes.

Somewhere out in the crowd I hear Kamos's deep voice say, "Lara from Earth make yourself orgasm for our pleasure."

I close my eyes and begin touching my clit. Rubbing it in circles and up and down. My other hand pulls at my nipple.

I hear someone yell, "Nine minutes left."

And the men start chanting, "Faster! Faster! Faster! Rub your fur human!"

But I can't do it. My body just won't. I bite my lower lip, open my eyes and look at the Octopod trader. He's angry. Bad things can happen to me if he loses too many UCs.

Gael forgive me. I think of Gael. I think of the way he looked naked at the sex temple. The way his hair swayed back and forth as he pounded into me. How alive I felt with him. How human I felt in his arms. Suddenly I'm there with Gael and not here at Gala. And it's not long before I can't hear anything. I don't hear the minutes counting down nor do I hear the alien males' chanting. It's quiet and there's Gael.

I'm coming so hard now I squirt out into the audience in front of me. It doesn't stop them from asking to touch my 'wet fur,' afterwards. I know I'm starting to come down from the drug because I feel ashamed. I feel guilty that I brought my memory of Gael here to this dirty place and to perform for these males who only see me as a stupid human pet.

I check the holographic clock. I orgasmed at five minutes and thirty seconds, so my Octopod trader still gets his five thousand for me.

Kamos addresses the Octopod trader again. "You can let these males caress the fur between her legs for one UC each and keep that. It's clear she still needs more training."

Two of the Octopod's assistants come out and I'm tied up by my wrists and ankles against a cross shaped stand. It's cold against my back. Then alien males begin lining up to pet me between my legs.

I want to go somewhere else in my head but at the same time I need to make sure Kamos still buys me, so I need to be present and play my part. I look at every male alien and I begin counting them as they stroke my wet hair as they pass. Most of them say things like, "What a good little human you are." But some say really terrible things like, "If you were mine, I would breed you to death. Look at all this blonde hair." Some of the aliens pull on my pubic hair hard enough for me to shout out in pain which everyone finds 'adorable.' Finally, when I think it's all over, everyone parts for a large man. He walks up escorted by two guards who are paradoxically considerably smaller than he is. He takes out a sword and runs it up and down my naked body. This is undoubtedly Kamos.

"Did you enjoy having so many males touch you, my pet?"

I don't answer because I don't know what to say.

One of the guards says, "Her Imperial may not be good enough to understand you."

Then he takes the tip of his sword and circles my nipple with it drawing some blood. He leans down and sucks on my bloody nipple so hard I want to cry out from the pain, but I don't. Instinct tells me to endure it. Then his other hand squeezes my other nipple so hard I worry it might be permanently damaged, but again I don't make a sound. When he's content, he rises, sheaths his sword and says, "Put her in the holding cell. I'm looking for five others as well. Not young ones, they cry."

I'm ushered off and put in a holding cell. It's pitch black. There's nowhere to sit and the floor feels filthy when I rub a foot along it, so I stand. I can't hear anything, so I only have my thoughts to keep me company. I move my ring along my finger. It feels of nothing now. I've never felt so alone as I do now in the darkness with my shame and fear. "Gael, I'm sorry I used your memory."

CHAPTER 17

GAEL

I watch as Lara is brought out for sale. It's disgusting to hear the comments being made about her. I want to mute the sound, but I can't. I have to hear what happens. I need to get control of myself. If she can stand up there and do this then I can watch it.

I feel relief when Kamos agrees to buy her. However, I knew it wouldn't be that easy. I make a hole in my table with my fist when she sings and takes off her clothing. I destroy the whole table when she orgasms for everyone. Then I punch twenty holes in my wall as males fondle her. By the time Kamos reaches her I'm so distraught I decide I must do physical exercise, or I'll burst from guilt. And not just regret of sending her to Gala but knowing that what she did for those males, in front of those males, was a turn on for me too, which I hate. It's my Imperial blood and I wish I could wash it from my DNA. But I can't unsee what she did. It's burned into my memory and I want to pleasure myself at the thought of it, which also makes me sick to my stomach.

I walk towards the gym, shedding my clothing without care in the hallways. Once I reach the gym, I'm naked and find a practice sword. I pick it up and begin sparring with a holo character. Not long after Seo enters the gym.

"I heard you were here."

"I needed some exercise."

"I understand. I saw what they did..."

I grunt an answer. I just want to fight. I can't articulate how remorseful I feel.

"How about we spar?"

I nod.

Seo takes off his clothes and picks up another practice sword.

"I'm not going to take it easy on you."

"I don't want you to. I'm just as angry as you are."

I want to tell him, 'I doubt it.' But instead, I swing hard.

He blocks my swing and pushes me off. "You know she charmed us all. It was shocking to see her," he pauses to swing at me. "To see her galactic public self."

I push him back. "It's not who she is."

Seo pushes me and I almost trip backwards. "No, it's not. It's who she was made to be to survive. But with us she was real."

I swallow hard. "She was herself. She was sweet and curious."

Seo takes this opportunity to swing fast and hard, causing me to backtrack. "And she was brave and compassionate to go back to being owned for Terra Ka's cause."

"She didn't have a choice."

"She did."

I strike hard and Seo falls to the ground.

Seo says, "Once she married you and was on the *Sisu* she was free."

"She made a promise."

"But she was still free, and she took the assignment."

I drop my sword and sit next to Seo. My hands are bloody from destroying the furniture in my quarters and I feel exhausted. "She did take it willingly, didn't she?" It's important to me to hear from someone else that I didn't force her to do this.

Seo puts a hand on my arm. "She did. And she will return and be her true self with us again."

Chapter 18

Lara

I'm transferred off of Gala surrounded by Imperial guards but not the ones from the official military that brought me here. Guards wearing navy blue and with an insignia I assume must be Kamos's. There are no other women with me, but I'd be a fool to think he only bought me. Most likely he wants to keep me separate from the others as a precaution. If I were him, I'd do the same. I wouldn't want a knowledgeable pet telling the others what's going to happen to them. That would ruin the surprise when they found out. And one thing I've learned in the galaxy is that alien males love to surprise their human pets.

I'm led on my leash into a transport and strapped in. No one makes eye contact or talks to me. It's all very bizarre given that I'd just been on a ship with Imperial people who treated me as an equal. And now I could pee all over the seat and they'd blame themselves for not thinking of my needs. It's like social whiplash and I have a moment where I question if Gael and Terra Ka even existed or was all of that a dream?

My mind can't resist the opportunity to think of Gael then. The first man who ever took my opinion into account since I left Earth. And he met me in the same condition as these men. But the difference was he wanted more than sex from me. But we still had sex, I can't keep those images of his naked body against mine from my mind now as much as I want to suppress them to keep them sacred. My mind refuses to lock them away.

It's not long before we are boarding a massive starship. There are Imperial men everywhere in the navy blue uniforms with Kamos's mark. I can make out bits and pieces of what they're saying but for the most part I'm ignorant. All I know right now is that I'm being taken to see a doctor.

No surprises there. Kamos will want to make sure for himself that I'm healthy. Everyone still remembers the human who purposely infected herself with a disease to kill her Imperial master. Lord Juo told me the story as evidence of how cruel Imperials are to humans. But alien males in the galaxy will say anything about humans to keep our status low so I don't know if that ever really happened.

The medical center is busy. I'm made to wait with the guard who's leading me around. He commands me to sit at his feet on the cold floor. It's degrading, but I do it. I take this opportunity to watch and learn. Everyone in the medical center is male which isn't surprising. In a matriarchal galaxy, women tend to make men go out and do their bidding while they stay on planet safe and sound.

After about 30 minutes the doctor says he'll see me. He doesn't talk to me of course, but the guard holding my leash. I'm led over to a semi-private medical bed and the guard doesn't hesitate when the doctor tells him to remove my clothing. He violently rips the gold clothing from my breasts and from between my legs.

The doctor comes over and strokes me between my legs how one would stroke a beloved pet. "That's a good girl. You know what to do. Up on the bed."

When I don't immediately respond, the doctor repeats himself.

The guard slaps my backside. “Up human. Up on the bed.”

I comply as if I didn’t know what was going on before and both the doctor and guard smile as if I’m a cute imbecile.

“Lie down,” the doctor commands.

I lie down and the doctor runs some scanners over me. He takes some blood. As he does a few passes he touches my breasts and nipples inappropriately. I can’t understand what he’s saying but my guard grunts.

Then the doctor pats the hair between my legs and says, “Stay.” Then he walks away.

I lie on the bed looking up at the grey ceiling wondering what’s happening now. I’m beginning to get cold and my whole body is covered in goosebumps, my nipples tight. I look over at my guard. He’s staring at me in a way that makes me wish I’d never looked over at him.

The doctor returns with a few other men. I hear the doctor say, “Here she is Lord Kamos. She is clean and healthy. There’s no trace of semen inside of her or any trace that she’s been entered for sex recently. Not that I would have expected much else from Lord Juo.”

I wonder for a second if I should sit up, but I decide against it. I continue lying down as if I don’t know what’s going on. Suddenly I feel a large cold hand between my legs spreading my thighs apart.

“Lara, my pet.”

I move my head to look at Kamos. He’s a hulking grey man with long black hair. He’s got grey eyes that look cruel. I don’t say anything as we make eye contact.

“Do you know any Imperial?”

“A little, Master.”

"Good," he says and strokes me strongly between my legs, purposely arousing me. "That's a good girl. You're clever so you'll learn Imperial, right?"

I nod.

With lightning speed he smacks me hard on my clit and I flinch. The pain spreads through my body in a nauseated wave.

"You will answer when I speak to you."

"Yes, Master."

He begins stroking me again. "Good girl. Listen I know that it'll cause you brain damage if I download Imperial into your translator or remove your Uru translator, so you have one month to learn Imperial well enough to function as my pet, or we will risk brain damage. You understand? One month."

My eyes must have revealed my shock. There's no way I can learn the rest of this language in one month. "I understand," I say but my voice becomes shaky.

"Oh my pet, see you're so bright you know I'll be true to my word and that's why you're scared. But I don't need a smart pet. I need a sexy pet. I need a pet that will follow instructions and you can't do that if you don't speak the language. And I'm impatient, you understand. One month or it's..." he makes a gesture of someone hitting me on the head.

I stop myself at the last minute from nodding and say, "I understand, Master."

He begins rubbing his thumb over my clit now. "Good girl. You want to orgasm for me again? You put on such a show at Gala. You're a good human aren't you? Always wanting to be touched."

I know I need to answer him but it's difficult, but I make myself say the words, "Yes, Master."

He continues stroking me as the doctor, the guard and all the other men watch. The doctor begins rubbing my nipples roughly and says something I don't understand.

I close my eyes.

"Lara open your eyes. Look at me."

My eyes meet Kamos's cruel grey ones, as he's bringing me closer and closer to orgasm, his hand moving vigorously across my sex. I'm arching my hips to meet the sensations.

"Have you ever been with an Imperial? Don't lie now. The doctor will know."

I can hardly think. There's no way I can lie in this pre-orgasmic state.

The doctor is still tugging on my breasts and interjects, "Look at these virgin nipples, of course she's not been with an Imperial."

I'm so close to orgasm. I have to concentrate on not closing my eyes.

"Lara," Kamos slaps me hard between my legs and pain and pleasure rush through my body. "Has an Imperial man entered you?"

"One time," I say in my accented Imperial.

"Just as I thought. Good girl."

Kamos stops touching me right before bringing me release and I'm devastated. "I'll finish this later. You are *not* to touch yourself and if you orgasm by rubbing your legs together, you'll be punished. You are not allowed to come until I tell you to."

"I understand, Master."

I watch Kamos and his men walk away. All I want to do is put my hands between my legs and get the release I need but both the doctor and the guard are looking at me. The doctor inserts something into my arm. He doesn't bother to tell me what it is. I assume it's a tracker. "Guard, please hold her."

I tense then, wondering what they're going to do to me. The guard holds both my arms down and the doctor grabs one of my nipples. I watch in horror as he pierces it. The discomfort and satisfaction are indescribable. Then he does my other nipple. Next, he uses a device to heal them completely. Now I have two large silver hoops through my nipples.

"Are we finished?" my guard asks.

The doctor turns and looks me up and down. "For now."

"Come on Lara," my guard says and rattles the chain around my neck.

I get off the medical bed and I try to pick up my ripped clothing from the floor, but he pulls me back with the chain.

"No. You don't need those now."

I wonder if I'm going to get any new clothing or if I'll be naked for my entire time here. I'd heard of some pets never getting any clothing.

My guard leads me through more hallways until we arrive in a washing area. There are two young Imperial men here and they look at me as I come in. "Oh, another one," the taller one says.

"She's the last and the most special. Be gentle with her."

"Oh we will," says the shorter one. "We're expert human pet groomers. Humans love the way we clean them."

I don't like the look in his eyes and I take a step behind my guard.

"Look you've frightened her already," my guard says.

"Come here little human. We won't hurt you," the taller man says as they both start walking towards me with their hands outstretched.

My guard brings me around and pushes me towards the men. "You be a good girl. They are going to clean all that Gala muck off of you."

I try to run but my guard catches my arm and says to the men, "She doesn't speak Imperial well. Be careful."

"You better stay," the shorter one says. "To hold her. The last one broke her head open trying to run and slipped on the soap."

My guard sighs but picks me up and takes me further into this washing area. I'm placed in a clear cylinder and lukewarm water begins to fall on me.

I scream a little because it's cold and I know soon I'll begin shivering.

The taller man gets some soap and begins lathering it all over my body. It smells like petrichor, and I turn up my nose at it.

The smaller one laughs. "They don't like the soap. Humans just want to be dirty don't you, my little darling? But we are going to make you a clean little Imperial pet. Stay still while we wash your fur. That's a good girl."

The taller one begins soaping my breasts and nipples more than he needs to and my body begins reacting to his touch. More than anything I still want to orgasm as I'm still heavily on edge, but at the same time I worry about Kamos's punishment. *How bad would it be?* I have no doubt that he would say I seduced these young men with my wild human pet ways. But my body is in agony with primal desire for release from anyone.

I stand completely still as the taller man cleans my nipples and moves my new nipple piercings back and forth and it's erotic. And I feel like I've always had the jewelry thanks to the doctor's ministrations. Back and forth my breasts are led. It feels so good. I open my mouth as a reaction to this new jewelry.

"She's not supposed to orgasm," my guard says.

The taller one stops caressing my breasts and I look at him with hungry eyes.

The smaller one puts his hand between my legs and begins moving it up and down with soap and I rock my hips to his motion.

"But humans love sex. It's all they want. They can't help themselves. And look at her. She wants this so much. It'd be a crime to not give her what she wants. Look how cute she is."

And he was right. I wanted this. I look up at my guard innocently. We hold eye contact as the smaller one begins vigorously rubbing me from the top of my sex to the bottom of my tailbone, circling my anus and the entrance to my core. The taller one resumes fondling my slippery soapy breasts. Their fingers feel so good against my skin. Moving so silkily and aptly with the soapy water. I'm so close.

"You're such a little minx," my guard says, "you're going to get me in trouble but it seems you can't help yourself. Come on, orgasm for us all then. Oh she's so close. That's a naughty human." Then he says to the other men, "You should have seen her in Gala. It was quite a show."

Seconds later I'm coming in the shower, my entire body vibrating with the muscle contractions from these men's hands over my cold wet body. Physically it feels amazing but when I open my eyes, it's emotionally empty. In fact, it stole some of my emotional grit from me.

Afterwards, as I'm being dried off, I can't help but wonder what my punishment will be and hope I haven't ruined my chances of being successful in my mission because of physical want. *Maybe they're right about humans? Maybe all we want is sex?*

I'm led into another area of this room where there are lots of small chains and clothes displayed in open wardrobes. The taller man and smaller man discuss their ideas about what I should be wearing before bringing out some clothing for me. They hold up different colors and then finally decide on a light pink dress. I look forward to it going over my body as I'm cold, but I'm horrified when I realize that the dress leaves my breasts, underarms, and sex completely exposed. Not only that, but the men begin to add oil to my breasts so that they shine. Next my hair is braided into two intricate braids and a silver ornament is attached with a chain that falls down my back. Next two ornate silver chains are attached to my nipples and then the one on the back of my chain is run through my legs and the folds of my sex to meet the chains going through my nipples.

"Not too tight," my guard says.

"She's the kind of pet who likes it tight. I doubt you'll be able to walk from here to Kamos's rooms without her coming again. Look she's so happy with the chain rubbing against her sex. Trust me I know humans." The taller one says rubbing the hair between my legs again and then looking at his work in the full-length mirror.

I am *not* happy. But people will see anything they want to especially when they're doing terrible things to others. I've seen that over and over again in my life. When the taller man moves away, I move my legs from side to side, to try and get comfortable with the silver chain rubbing against my pelvic bone. I try to pull it down to give myself a little breathing room, but then I inadvertently pull on my nipples. "Oh," I say in surprise.

"Loosen it," my guard says, and the taller man finally complies.

Once my guard is satisfied, I'm led to a kind of kitchen where I'm given food and water. I'm not allowed to eat the food myself. My guard feeds it to me as the chef sits next to me and plays with the chain attached to my nipples. It's difficult for me to concentrate on eating as the chain that connects my nipples and then across my pelvic bone is being yanked and played with. As soon as I get the chance I'm going to push for more medicine in my arm.

But I need to save that for my punishment with Kamos, I remind myself.

When my guard thinks I've eaten enough, I assume we're going to leave the kitchen, but the chef asks if he can have a few seconds with me. I don't understand everything he says, but it seems like he and my guard are friends and so the guard agrees. The chef begins touching my underarms and pulling at my hair there. Then between my legs. When he puts a finger inside of my sex I give a little whimper.

"No, Kamos will have her first. Not even a finger."

"Apologies," says the chef as he licks the finger that was just inside of me and then he moves his hands to run the length of my torso and weighing out my breasts in his hands.

My guard says something and then the chef pats me on the head and we leave the kitchens. I feel awkward walking these hallways dressed like this with a leash with Imperial people that look like Gael's crew, but see me as non-sentient. It was easier to play the role of a pet with large tentacled aliens that could easily kill me if they weren't gentle. Imperials are the same species as I am. Yet I have to play along with this kinky farce because my skin is not grey.

As we walk through the hallways all the Imperial men seem to notice me now. I guess the outfit is the signal I'm a pet and they can all stop and grope me. And they do. We've hardly walk ten meters and I'm feeling like I could orgasm again with the number of grey hands touching my exposed body. My guard and I are surrounded by men all in navy-blue uniforms, touching me. I feel like I have 50 fingers on me, pinching my nipples, petting my pubic hair, and all calling me a "good human pet."

I'm so close to coming again. One of them is yanking the chain on my nipples, which is also rubbing against my engorged folds. I move my hips from side to side to get the chain to rub in a rhythm that feels good. I can't help myself. I orgasm again for these men and they all pet me on my head and between my legs and tell me, "Good human pet." Again, I've lost more emotional grit. I've only been here an hour and I'm already being broken down into my place.

This is how my life always was before Gael. Empty touches with only physical release which becomes addictive. With Gael I experienced emotional desire. I was actually attracted to the man. Not only did I want him to touch me, but I also wanted to touch him too. I have never wanted to touch any other man in the galaxy and certainly none of these Imperial men which is reassuring. One of the things I worried about was whether or not I liked Gael just because he was Imperial and seemed to like me. But it turns out, I like Gael because I'm attracted to him, not just because he looks like a human with grey skin.

Finally, we reach Kamos's rooms. There are guards at the door, but they quickly open the doors for us. I'm led into opulent rooms not unlike what I was accustomed to with Lord Juo. I'm taken to an area that has little cages and am placed in an empty one. It has a little bed, only big enough for me to curl up on and a jug of water that I can sip like an animal. My guard takes off my chain and puts me in the cage.

"Toilet?" I ask.

He points to a little mat in my cage. "You can use that." And then closes the shiny door.

I sit on the little bed and eye the women in the cages to my left and right. They are looking at me too. I don't recognize either of them from Gala so they must have been with Kamos awhile which is convenient. Maybe they can help me.

"So you're both here too," I say in English when we are alone.

A woman with dark brown hair and strong green eyes answers me, "I'm Coco. That's Ava," she points to the woman on the other side of me.

"I'm ..."

"We know," Ava says. "Lara from the other side of the galaxy."

"It's been all anyone has been talking about for the last hour. Did you work as a sex worker on Earth first?" Coco asks.

"Why do you ask that?"

"We heard about your show at Gala. Who performs like that at a slave market?"

I feel ashamed of my behavior momentarily. "I was abducted by the Dulu at the age of eight and have been with Lord Juo ever since then. Well, almost."

"Almost?" Coco asks suspiciously.

"I spent a few days at the Fertility Temple."

"Never heard of it," says Ava.

"Me neither."

"It's on the other side of the galaxy. It's basically a sex temple. I was dropped there by the IGC after my master died," I explain trying to gain some sympathy so I can get information from them.

"Wait a second," Ava says. "Were you free?"

"I was a ward of the temple nuns."

"How did you get to Gala? Were you stolen?"

"I was misled." I concentrate on my story and try to make it as simple and as close to the truth as possible. "A man named Gael..."

"Gael the Returner?" Coco asks, her voice slightly louder.

"Yes."

"He *rescued* you?"

"Not exactly. He had sex with me so that I could leave the temple and then he set me free but I don't have any skills but this. So I allowed myself to be sold again."

"Gael has sex with everyone. He had sex with me," Coco says and my heart shatters.

"Were you lovers?"

"Of a kind," Coco says.

"How is that possible if you're a pet for Kamos?"

"I chose to be here too. Kamos and I have something special. Gael and I never had that. Gael is weak."

"You love Kamos?" I ask.

"You'll see," says Ava putting her brown hair behind her ears. "He's a good master."

"Freedom is complicated," I say. "I thought I wanted it..."

Coco looks away as if I've said something to upset her.

"I'm not fooled by the idea of being free," Ava says. "Like you, I've been a pet for a long time. Kamos has given me the best life and it's a life of luxury I could never have elsewhere. Not on Earth and not as a *free* human anywhere else in the galaxy."

"But the laws have changed. You could be free to choose to be a pet if you wanted. I feel like I chose to be a pet now. My only wish is that I could choose to be another male's pet if I don't like Kamos's style of ownership."

"It's a law that no one respects," Coco says. "And we can never go back to Earth..."

"But it's still the law and if we fight for it we really could be free. Humans could choose how we want to live in the galaxy. I don't see a future where anyone would stop a human from being anyone's pet."

Ava waves her hand at me and Coco laughs. "It's a lost cause. Only a few Imperial religious zealots uphold the law. And even from your own experience, you should've been free when the IGC picked you up, but even they couldn't bear to let a human walk free."

"I hope you're not going to cause trouble for the rest of us," Coco says. "We have a good life here."

I let the topic drop and then change the subject. "I'm happy to hear that Kamos is a good master. I'd never met an Imperial before Gael." Mentioning Gael's name makes my stomach tighten. *Does he sleep with every woman before he sends them to Kamos?* I try to push down my embarrassment by believing I was special to him.

"Kamos is better than most Imperials," Coco tells me. "He's not a religious zealot and he actually keeps his children with him at his palace for a while."

"He doesn't live on this ship?"

"Only half the time. The other half, he's at home with his pets."

"No wives?"

"No, he likes humans," Ava says.

"How many human pets does he have?"

"About a hundred. But we are ranked. I'm number one. Ava is number three and you now are the new number two."

"What happened to the old number two?"

"I don't know," Coco says decidedly.

"Was she killed?"

"We don't know," Ava says strongly to get me to drop it.

"I'm nervous about being owned by an Imperial. I've only pleased Agnorrians and Uru before. The only man that's ever penetrated me with a human-like penis is Gael and I don't know if that was normal."

"Where did he put his dick? Did he try to put it in your ear or something?" Ava asks.

"No, it just never felt that way before." I close my eyes and I can still remember what it felt like having Gael inside of me. The warmness and naturalness of it. "It felt more real," I say bearing my heart in an effort to make a connection.

"It's because he was your first real man. Tentacles don't count. That's just disgusting wet tickling," Ava comments.

Coco looks especially interested now. "Haven't you ever been with a human man? It's almost the same."

"No. I was abducted as a girl. It's been 15 years since I saw a human in the flesh and then only women and girls at Gala."

Ava licks her lips. "Kamos likes to breed new pets to his liking with human men. So I'm sure he'll breed you too with a blonde man."

"He keeps men too?"

"No, he pays their owners to bring them to have sex with us and they all watch. It's humiliating for everyone except the spectators."

"I turn off my emotions or at least I try to. It was easier with tentacles touching me and alien males that looked nothing like humans."

"It's almost impossible when it's a man," says Coco. "It's like your body instantly recognizes what's happening."

"I was given to an Octopod once. I felt like I was playing at the beach. I couldn't take it seriously until one of his tentacles broke off inside of me and then it had to be removed by a doctor. I vomited repeatedly." She gags again at the thought.

"Even the memories of it and the smell. I asked to be bathed for hours afterward. Did aliens leave their tentacles in you?" Ava asks me with horror.

"No. No male had ever put anything in me before Gael. My last master was very protective of his property."

"You let..." before Ava could finish, the door to the rooms opened.

"Shhh..." Coco whispers. "They don't like it when we talk with each other. It's best to pretend to be asleep."

Coco and Ava curl up on their little beds and close their eyes. I decide to take their advice and follow suit. As I lie there, I hear Kamos and a few other men walk in. I can't make out all of their words, but it's clear we're well on our way to his palace which will take a day or two to reach. Gael made sure I knew the words 'teleportation suit,' so I have my ears on alarm for any mention of it. However, at the moment they're only talking about the human women and girls at Gala.

"I bought those babies to give to Gael the Returner."

"Why are you so nice to him, Kamos?"

"Only the truly sick want babies. Gael will see that they get back to Earth and kill those specific Dulu traders, and then we'll both look good."

Gael is in contact with Kamos? I remind myself that they don't have to be in direct contact. I know from the time I spent on the *Sisu* that Gael has a lot of people that deal with his communications and I assume it's the same for Kamos.

"They were *very* young," a man with a deep voice agrees. "One year old. I hardly agree with Gael's mission, but this time, I'm in full agreement of sending those human babies back and killing those Dulu."

They're speaking in galactic years so that's about three Earth years. I'm with Kamos and the mysterious deep voice, that's disgusting to take children so young. Not that any age is okay, but it seems even criminals like Kamos have their moral limits.

"It's well-known only the Octopods and their ilk want humans so young to groom them into vessels for their offspring or other curiosities," another man says with an Imperial accent that sounds different from the others.

"Speaking of which," Kamos says, "Let's check on my newest addition from the other side of the galaxy. I'm sure she's going to have some kinks from being with all those tentacled aliens I'll enjoy breaking her of."

I hear footsteps coming towards our cages. I try to remain still and keep my breathing slow, but my heart is beating a mile a minute. *Is he going to punish me now for orgasming not once but twice after he left me in the medical center?*

I hear my cage open and hands reach in to take me out. I allow it to happen and open my eyes to find Kamos holding me like a baby.

"There you are. You're so clean now like a good Imperial pet. But I see just as scared." He pulls a little on the chain connected to my nipples and my eyes widen. "It must be such a new sensation. But you're with your own people now. We'll treat you well." He walks me over into a different room, the other men, who I assume must be officers by their uniforms follow. Once there I'm laid down on top of a table. The two men stand to each side as Kamos lifts up my pink dress. I don't know why he needs to, my breasts and sex are on display either way. But I realize at the last minute he has something in his hand and I try to squirm away because it looks like a weapon.

Kamos grabs my thigh and holds it tightly to the table. His men hold me down as well.

"If you struggle this will only take longer," Kamos says as he brings the weapon down to my lower abdomen.

I scream as the pain radiates through my body. I smell my flesh burning. As soon as it's over, the men all release me, and I sit up. I've been branded like livestock with Kamos's insignia. I put my hand down to touch it and it hurts. I wince from the hot pain.

This seems so permanent and so extremely real. I know I'll hopefully be going back to Gael and Hela can erase this with modern medicine, but what if that never happens? I was never marked before. I keep up the mantra in my mind that it'll be removed later, but I can't help it, I begin to cry.

"It's for your protection so if you get lost you'll be returned to me, pet," Kamos says, stroking my hair.

I am not your pet, I think. But I say nothing because I am his pet and if I don't escape with that teleportation suit, I'll be his property forever. I try to wipe my tears and go away with my mind like I used to easily be able to do but I can't. My mind and my attention won't budge from this situation. Why am I even here if Kamos is sending humans back anyway? Have I been tricked? Has Gael lied to me? Did he lie to Coco and that's why she is still here? Did he legitimately sell me and I was too trusting and too ignorant to realize it?

I can't believe that. However, I don't have time to think about that because Kamos picks me up and is carrying me back to the other room with Coco and Ava. He instructs his men to get them out of their cages and lines us all up naked except our leashes attached to our nipples.

I am in the second position standing between the two women. They stand looking forward and I try to do the same, but I've too many negative thoughts in my mind to look ahead. My head keeps looking at the branding and salty tears are dripping off my face.

"See Lara, look at Coco and Ava, they also have my mark. You should be honored."

I don't look. My tears continue to fall.

"Lara do you understand?"

I force myself to look at Ava and Coco's brands. They look the same as mine. "I understand," I say with a shaky voice.

"Stop crying. I don't tolerate crying."

"Yes, Master."

"Now I want you to kiss Coco's brand and then Ava's brand."

I do as Kamos says. I move over to Coco. I bend down and kiss her brand. Unlike mine that's red and angry, hers is healed over. Then I move over to Ava and do the same.

"Good girl," Kamos says. "Now get back in line. I want to compare your body to Coco and Ava's." Kamos walks in front of me and holds one of my breasts in his hand and with his other he holds Coco's and then Ava's. "Nice large tits," he says. "Now all of you bend over and hold yourselves open. I want to see both holes."

I turn and bend over. I hold my sex open for his inspection. I can feel Kamos walk behind me, his finger trailing over my tailbone and then down into my vagina.

"Lara is always wet," he says. "That's a good human. And so much fur. You're going to be a pleasure to breed."

Then I feel his finger enter my anus. I immediately tighten.

"Open up for me Lara. Soon there'll be something bigger in there."

I feel him move his finger back and forth and I try to do as he says but I don't know how. But soon he takes his finger away saying, "We have some work do to, but it will be fun for all of us. Stand up and face me."

We all stand back up.

"Coco and Ava, get your ball and play with Lara. I can't have this weeping."

Coco and Ava don't bother putting on their clothing but hurry across the room to get a rainbow colored ball and they begin passing it to one another and then to me. At first the ball just hits me hard in the chest and falls to the ground. I've never played with a ball before.

Coco using a completely different tone than her true tone in the cage says in Imperial, "Pick it up and play. Play!"

I tentatively pick up the ball and throw it as hard as I can.

"Ouch," Ava says as I made one of her nipple piercings bloody with the force of my throw.

"Sorry," I say quickly.

"Lick it better," Kamos commands from the other side of the room.

I make eye contact with Ava. She doesn't seem surprised at all by this. I walk across the soft rug to Ava and lean down to take her small breast and bloody nipple into my mouth. I gently lick the blood on the nipple.

"Suck," says Kamos.

I open my mouth and lightly suck. I feel her nipple ring in my mouth and her nipple get hard. I don't stop until Kamos tells me to. I feel like it's an eternity before I'm given the signal.

"That's enough. I don't want you humans getting too excited. Get back to your ball game."

"Not so hard," Coco instructs me handing me the ball. I take it and throw it so lightly it almost falls to the floor before Coco can catch it.

We play with the ball while Kamos and his men talk. I try to listen at the same time as *playing* with Coco and Ava but it's not easy.

This time the ball accidentally hits me on my nipple because I looked away from the game when I heard the words, 'teleportation suit.' And it's proof that Kamos is keeping a close eye on us because he then makes Ava come over and suck on my nipple even though it isn't bleeding.

"See you both are even now," Kamos says and then returns to his conversation.

After playtime, guards come in and lead us by our nipple leashes to a dining area. We are still naked, and the chair is cold against my backside. Very plain food is laid out for us, and we're each spoon fed by our own individual guard. I notice that I have more food than Coco and Ava. Because of that they all have to wait for me to finish.

After mealtime we are led back to our cages and told to sleep.

I'm not tired, but close my eyes obediently and hope Kamos has forgotten about my punishment.

"Come on little pets," I hear a guard say as my cage is opened. "We're home."

Rough hands lift me out of my cage and a leash is returned to my nipple rings. The pull feels uncomfortable. My leash is attached to Coco and Ava's and we're led out of Kamos's rooms. The hallways are busy with people preparing to disembark.

I've no idea what to expect from Kamos's palace. I've heard so many conflicting things. What I didn't expect was a picturesque fortress in the middle of a desert. But there it is before me. A desert palace with large yellow stone walls lined with windows. Above the palace is a heavy defense forcefield and I can see small fighters all protecting his prized palace. *How am I ever going to escape?*

Light blue sunlight covers the planet giving everything a blueish tint. "Where are we?" I ask in a whisper.

"Kamos's palace," Coco says as if I must have hit my head really hard.

"No, I mean where in the galaxy."

"I have no idea," replies Coco. "I don't even know Earth's address."

"Me neither," whispers Ava.

"No talking," the guard in front of Coco says evenly.

As we are led into the palace my bare feet rejoice on the warm stone tiles. Being barefoot on spaceships is the worst, it's as if your feet are always numb from the cold floors.

Our guard leads us through exquisite stone corridors with painted murals and various courtyards of charming gardens. I can smell flowers and earth. It's now been months since I've been on a planet and all my senses are rejoicing.

Finally we are led through large ornamental gates with more guards. I see some of the other women from Gala in front of us. They're all being stripped of their clothing and jewelry.

I finger my ring from Gael. No matter how lavish this palace is, I must always remember it's a prison. As I watch the women in front of us, I think about swallowing my ring and then finding it later in my poo. It's my only option to hide it.

I stand in the line as female guards frisk all the women in front of us. However, when they see Coco and Ava we're waved through without a search. I breathe a quiet sigh of relief. I've never swallowed anything to look for later, and this ring's stone looks sharp.

Our guard takes us into a very grand sitting room with perfectly patterned large mashrabiya windows that lets in some of the blue sunlight. The furniture looks invitingly comfortable with organic patterns on bright colors. I hardly notice as our leashes are removed and once again we are free.

Our guard leaves without a word, but before I'm free to explore on my own, a large Imperial female approaches me. "You're Lara from Lord Juo?"

"Yes."

"I'm the head guard in the harem," she says and then clamps a heavy bracelet around my left wrist. "If you leave the palace grounds that will poison you and send out a beacon for us to find you. If we find you in time you won't die. Understand?"

"I understand. What planet are we on?"

She shakes her head at me. "Just don't leave. When one of you dies we all suffer Kamos's rage especially if it's one of his alphas."

"What do you mean, alphas?"

The head guard motions to the stunning room around us with her finger. "This area is for alphas and your bedrooms. It's more luxurious than the rest of the harem and you've access to more servants, better food, and more UCs to buy appropriate clothing and jewelry for your position. There are only three alphas at any time."

"And the other women?"

"They are segregated into betas and deltas. Six betas and nine deltas. You can socialize with them in other areas of the harem, but never forget they're less than you."

"What's expected of me?"

"To serve Kamos in whatever way he wants. To keep yourself clean and your body and mind healthy."

"That's all?"

"And not to cause trouble. If you do there'll be punishments."

"I heard Kamos keeps his children here?" I ask out of curiosity.

"Yes." Just as the head guard is answering, I spot a little grey girl peek out and look at us from behind a wall. She's wearing a cute yellow dress. "That's Ava's daughter. Yes, the children are here until Kamos decides their futures."

"How does he do that?"

"That's not for us to think about. Now, follow me to your room. The last woman's things are still there. You may go through her belongings and see if you want anything. If not I'll offer it to the others."

"The last number two, did she die?"

"I don't know."

I'm led into a gorgeous set of rooms including a sitting room, a small dining area, a bathroom and a large bedroom. Everything is colorful and it has a pleasing floral scent. I run my hands over the engraved wooden table. "All of this is lovely."

"I'm glad. I was a bit concerned you might be disappointed after coming from Lord Juo's, he was very wealthy."

I don't answer her and she begins opening the wardrobes that are filled with silky clothing and various kinds of silver jewelry. I also can't miss all the leashes hanging in a special area along with whips.

"What are those for?" I point to the whips.

"Kamos likes to keep all his pets in order. If he wants to spank you for a small transgression you will bring your whip in your mouth to his rooms and he will use it on you. Speaking of which, you have to get better at Imperial or Kamos will force the doctors to implement it. I've seen that before and trust me, you don't want that."

"What happened?"

"The woman became mute and just did what anyone told her to do no matter what it was. It was very sad. She was gone inside. Don't let that happen to you. Learn Imperial as fast as you can. Your servant will help you. She's a very clever and patient young woman."

The head guard then introduces me to my own servant. A young Imperial woman with shoulder length hair who calls herself Rae.

"I'm here to serve."

"Thank you. I'd like some food," I say testing the waters.

Rae nods and disappears.

The head guard gives me one final look and then says, "Behave yourself, learn Imperial, and you'll be happy here, Lara from Earth."

I don't say anything, but her tone reminds me again of Kamos's threat of a punishment although her words were meant to be kind.

As the head guard leaves, my servant Rae enters with dishes of food. She goes into the little dining room and sets them down and then calls me over. I almost have whiplash from being treated like a real pet by the male guards to a sentient guest by the female guards. Although Rae calls herself a 'servant,' I'm under no illusion that she isn't just as much a guard as the head guard herself.

I sit down and thank Rae for the food. Then I ask, "Where do you sleep?"

She seems surprised by the question. "In your room, of course. I'm here for your every need no matter what time of day."

"What do you know about my punishment?"

Our eyes meet and her grey ones search mine. "I know it's scheduled to begin tomorrow."

"Begin?"

She makes me repeat the word, 'begin, 'corrects my pronunciation and then answers my question, "Yes. It will last three days."

"What's my punishment?"

"Your right wrist and right ankle will be chained to Coco and your left hand and left ankle will be chained to Ava. Kamos never punishes anyone alone. We are all a collective and when one person steps out of line it creates a ripple in our serenity. Everyone most immediately touched by that ripple is punished."

"Do Coco and Ava know they'll be punished with me tomorrow?"

"I'm sure their servants have told them by now," she says casually. "Now," she says picking up a spoon, "Let me feed you."

"No, I'm capable."

"It's not about being capable. You've been described as the perfect human pet and I don't want to ruin anything for Kamos. Please let me feed you."

I indulge her. The more obedient I am, the less I'll be suspected of being a spy. "What's the perfect human pet?"

"You."

"How?"

Her hand grasps one of my breasts and bounces it up and down. "You have the perfect size breasts for a human. Big enough to move with all of your movements but not too big that they are obscene." Then she caresses the hair under my arms. "And you have a good amount of human fur that's never been cut."

"What do you mean, 'never been cut?'"

"Most of the humans taken from Earth have either cut their fur or had it permanently removed which decreases their attractiveness."

"Is that all?"

"You have a high sex drive which Kamos looks forward to teaching you how to control. It's one of the things he enjoys most with his human pets, the training."

"Have you seen many pets trained?"

"A few," she says and then begins stroking the hair between my legs. I want to cross my legs and tell her not to touch me there, but I'm here as a spy and the less she suspects me the better. So, I open my legs wider.

Rae smiles. "See this is why Kamos wants to break you. You want to be touched. You don't shy away like other human pets. You want to be noticed by your master."

"It feels so good," I say because I know it's what she wants to hear.

Rae doesn't stop touching me. "It's satisfying to watch your face flush as you enjoy yourself which is the final thing that makes you the perfect human pet."

"I was always told my skin color was an abomination."

"Not here. You were on the wrong side of the galaxy where you couldn't be appreciated." Rae pats my pubic hair and then says, "And you'll be bred."

"With human men?"

"I don't know. It's up to Kamos to decide. You're his."

"I'm sorry," I whisper to Coco and Ava as we are chained together. "If I'd known I would've tried harder to resist. I thought the punishment would be my own."

They don't give me any acknowledgement of hearing me.

Once we are all bound and large butt plugs are wedged tightly in our rears the head guard says, "For the next three days, you'll go wherever the most important of you wants or must go, which is of course Coco. If Coco incurs a punishment while you three are together, you will all suffer that as well. If you need the bathroom, then you all go together and clean each other. You will all sleep together. Right now Coco has an appointment so walk carefully and follow me."

We all walk slowly together through the hallways that barely fit the three of us across. All the women in the harem stop to look at us as we pass. The head guard reminds them, "This is what happens when you disobey Kamos. Take note of their punishment. Everything they do they will do chained together for the next three days without any privacy: eat, drink, bathe, use the toilet, and be good sexual pets."

I make eye contact with some of the women and the ones I recognize from Gala have a look of horror on their faces as we walk by, our chains making a sound with every step we take.

Coco, Ava, and I walk slowly for about 15 minutes, out of the harem's large gates and then four guards join us as we make our way to a completely different area of the palace. I want to ask where we're going but I've learned to keep my mouth shut outside the harem. No one likes their pets speaking unless spoken to.

Finally, we enter a green room without any furniture but it has strange rugs covering the floor. The rugs are very soft and my feet melt into them. We are told to stop and wait in the center of the large room. We stop. The doors are shut loudly behind us and we are alone.

"What's going on?" I whisper.

Both women shake their heads at me.

Then after a few minutes an Imperial man with a black uniform comes in with a human man on a leash and Kamos and a few of Kamos's officers.

"Why are there three?"

"Oh it's punishment. I've a new pet and she must be trained. The one on the right is for your pet."

This is my first time seeing a human man in the flesh since I was eight years old. I'm fascinated by his light brown skin and his thick dark hair that curls at the ends. His body is also covered in body hair and I'm surprised that not only is he this way but that I've the urge to run my hands through his body hair. *I am just as bad as Imperials,* I chide myself.

The Imperial man walks over to the three of us and eyes us all up and down. "What about we change it for the one in the middle?" He touches me between my legs. "She's already even wet."

"No. We decided on Coco and it'll be Coco or no one." Kamos walks over to stand on Coco's side. He runs his hands over her breasts to make her nipples hard. "See she's just as attractive when aroused."

The Imperial man turns his attention towards Coco and puts his hands between her legs. He makes her stand with her legs apart and then turn, meaning we all have to turn and bend over when asked. "Do you mind if I look at the other two?"

Kamos must have agreed because I feel the man spreading my butt cheeks apart and playing with the butt plug. He takes it out and then runs a finger around my anus. I can't help but be curious about the strange sensations coursing through my body. Then I hear him spit and feel the butt plug go back in. Then he moves to Ava and must do the same because she makes a moan of pleasure and I hear the man spit again.

The men in the room are all talking about our different bodies. Comparing our breast sizes and the curve of our hips. I've never been in a room with so many of my same species. I know better than anyone here, that we are all the same species, grey skin, brown skin, my pinkish pale skin, all my instincts tell me we are the same. So it's ridiculous this whole pet charade.

When he's fully examined Coco again he says, "Fine. I just want to make sure my pet enjoys this too. It's cruel to show him these other two beauties he can't have."

"I'm sure he won't mind," Kamos says decidedly. Then to us he says, "Lay down, my sweet pets. Open your legs Coco, you're going to get a treat."

Coco and Ava are faster than I am to lay on their backs on the soft floor. There's no need to remove any of our clothing as our breasts, underarms, and sexes are completely exposed.

The human man still wearing black underwear stands over us. He has a leash around his neck. He's looking at me with hungry eyes and although I'm curious how his hairy body would feel next to mine, it's nothing but sheer curiosity and lust.

"No, Jon," his master says. "This one on the right. Down. Put your mouth on her clit just like we practiced."

The man gets on his knees and obeys. He begins licking Coco between her legs while the Imperial men look on and judge his skills. They all come to the conclusion human men need training in cunnilingus.

Coco begins to come close to climaxing and the human man takes off his underwear. Then he's beaten with a whip by his master who says, "She's not ready. She must orgasm first. Bad boy."

The human man makes eye contact with me before putting his head between Coco's legs again. His lips are glossy with Coco's desire and I feel primeval. I want this human man to do the same to me and I don't know if I want it because it won't happen or if I want it because he's human.

"Your human is trying to rush things," Kamos says, clearly not pleased with the man's performance.

"He's new. I've only had him for a few months. He hardly speaks Imperial. But once he gets going he's a real stallion. You just wait and see."

I feel Coco getting close to her orgasm. Her body is tense and she's moaning a bit. I look up at the green ceiling and wonder if this could get any stranger. Finally Coco comes in a wave of spasms and she brings her hands to her breasts to caress them. Which means my hand follows too.

The human man makes eye contact with me again and then puts my hand on Coco's breast. He pulls down his underwear and reveals a large brown penis surrounded by a lot of black hair. I stare. His penis is smooth all around not like an Imperial man's.

"Gorgeous," Kamos says. "Look at all that fur. They will have wonderful furry babies."

The human man never stops looking at me as he puts his large penis at the entrance of Coco. She spreads her legs for him even wider and he begins moving in and out of her, rattling all of our chains. The faster he pumps the faster all of our breasts move in unison with his movements due to us all being on the same bit of rug and the more Coco moans with satisfaction. I push my thighs together because despite the awkwardness of this situation, my body possibly affected by the smell of a human man, I want sex with him too. And I'd attempt to touch myself, but my hands are not free and it's forbidden, anyway. Only Kamos is allowed to say when we can orgasm. I know that I'll keep this memory of the hairy human man pumping into Coco as one of my tricks to get myself to orgasm on command in the future.

"They all want some of your pet," Kamos says.

"He's a good specimen. I've never seen a human woman yet to not open for him. We could do all three now?"

"No," Kamos says reluctantly. "I know they'd all like it, but the middle one still isn't trained and the one on the end isn't fertile now."

"It could be a reward for good behavior for the one on the end? She looks like a good pet."

"It's too much of a reward now, but in the future we'll bring him back if he breeds Coco."

The human man finishes with large groans and shakes while he fills Coco with his semen. I watch in fascination and he makes some final thrusts. Then he opens his eyes, he looks at me and licks his lips seductively.

I must have given him some signal without realizing. Suddenly, before his master can pull him back, he's hovering over my face and is forcing his wet cock into my mouth. I've had a lot of tentacles in my mouth before so I know how to take his big organ in without gagging. I taste the salty taste of human sex. I've never tasted anything like it and my curiosity devours his smooth human penis, the tangy taste of human sex, and the copious amounts of hair surrounding his sex touching my face. *Is this what human sex is like? Is this how humans begin or end?*

I hear Kamos and his master laugh. Then the human man is pulled off of me.

"She was a curiosity for Uru and Agnorrians and has some bad habits," Kamos explains. "I think she'd suck on anything you put near her mouth."

"And human men," the Imperial man says. "They'd put their penises anywhere to be sucked off."

The human man is moved away from us. I can see him in another area of the room. His master takes his heavy whip and beats the man's back for putting his penis in my mouth. Then he's given some water. It's unreal that we are all here, but none of the humans are allowed to speak. We just obey. And I don't know why we do. I conclude in the silence that I must find some comfort and pleasure in all of this.

Coco, Ava, and I just lie still. I push my thighs together and run my tongue over the taste of the human man's semen and Coco's desire in my mouth trying to work out the tastes.

Surprisingly a doctor comes in and pets Coco as he examines her with his hand-held machine. He tells Kamos that there's no need to do it again.

"If it's going to happen there are enough viable sperm to seduce her egg, but it's all about whether the egg wants to be seduced by the sperm."

I don't understand everything the doctor has said. I know the words but it doesn't make sense to me.

Soon everyone leaves and the three of us are still lying on the soft floor looking at the ceiling. When I'm sure we are alone I ask, "How long do we have to stay here?"

"An hour or so," says Coco.

"Have you done this before?"

"Yes, but it didn't work. My egg didn't want the other man."

"Do you think it'll work this time?"

"I don't know. I can't control it. I did find this man much more attractive and he smelled good to me. I'm sure that has something to do with it. But I don't know how attractive he found me as he kept looking at you."

"I'm sorry. I had never seen a human man before. I didn't expect him to be so hairy and his penis so smooth."

"You sound like an Imperial," Ava says.

"She can't help it," Coco defends me. "She's been across the galaxy with tentacles. It's amazing she still speaks English."

"How do you speak English if you were the only human and abducted at eight years old? It's a well-known fact you lose languages you don't use when you go through puberty."

"Lord Juo made sure I had entertainment from Earth, and I had an AI to speak with."

"That must have been a lonely existence," Coco remarks.

"In all that entertainment you never saw a naked human man?" Ava asks.

"No. There was never any sex ever. Maybe a kiss or an allusion to an affair. That's why it's so odd that twice I've heard Imperial people say humans love sex. Why do they think this?"

Both women laugh at me.

"I don't know what's so funny."

"I shouldn't be laughing, I don't think. I want to be pregnant. But we're laughing because Earth is known for making lots of entertainment about sex. Possibly more than anywhere else in the galaxy. That's why they think humans are obsessed with sex and maybe we are?"

"Oh," I say. "My entertainment choices must have been censored."

"No doubt. Your master probably didn't want you to know what you were missing."

"Probably," I agree. Then after a few minutes of silence I say, "But it didn't work because I knew what I was missing even if I couldn't articulate it. I could feel it in my skin. Nothing was satisfying like a humanoid penis, although I've only experienced that once."

"Oh you'll have a lot more dick here," Coco laughs.

"When that man put himself in your mouth, did it feel right?" Ava asks curiously.

"I don't know. I can still taste him. It didn't feel as wrong as tentacles and their sour genetic material."

"Ewww 'sour genetic material,'" Coco says. "Stop making me laugh."

"I hope for your sake Lara that Kamos finds you a really lovely human man."

"Coco," I say more seriously. "Why do you want to be pregnant with that man's child?"

"I'm not getting any younger and it gives me better status. Also just look at Ava with her daughter. I want to experience love like that at least once."

"But is Ava's daughter going to be sold?" I feel the room instantly become colder. "I'm sorry I didn't mean..."

Neither woman says anything, and we lay in silence again.

Coco breaks the stillness. "Love comes and goes anyway. Why shouldn't I want love for a child even if it's not permanent? I still always will have had that time."

"For 15 years I lived in a luxurious zoo. I don't know anything about love, but I thought from what I read that when you fell in love with someone it was forever."

"It can be," Ava says. "But people you love can't be around forever even if they want to be."

"So then what happens."

"You miss them," Coco says. "It hurts like nothing else. Probably like it hurt when you missed your parents. You must have loved them."

I remember with acute clarity. I touch my arm for the medicine from Hela to give me strength. "It felt like I couldn't breathe I missed them so much in the beginning."

"That's love," says Coco. "It's the same with children."

"More with children. I'd die for Mei," Ava says.

We are quiet again. Everyone knows Mei's time is numbered in the harem. She has grey skin and looks Imperial. She can't stay.

"I want to be a mother even if I can only care for the child until she becomes an adult," Coco says.

Thoughts are swirling around in my head with this. "You don't mind the child will be born into captivity and live as a pet?"

"It's a better life than elsewhere and look at that man who just had sex with me. Our offspring will be a prince among pets."

The phrase, 'A prince among pets' floats through my mind and I am speechless.

(FIVE MONTHS LATER)

I open my eyes to Rae's quiet movements in my chambers. She's preparing to wake me up. Everything is calm and stable in the harem. But being a pet in Kamos's harem is a strange way to live. While I'm in the harem I feel almost free. I have everything I could want and I'm even able to choose the food I eat and the clothing I wear. Although there's a particular fashion and hierarchy I must adhere to within these locked doors. However, when I'm in other parts of the palace, I'm treated as a beloved, non-sentient pet. It's during those times I wonder if I have a split personality. How can I endure being treated like a sex object with no higher thoughts or emotions and then hours later talk about the meaning of life with other human women in the harem? I don't know the answer to this.

In the first weeks at the palace, I felt uncomfortable and disappointed in myself for accepting this double-sided life. But as my Imperial has become more fluent and I developed relationships with the other women both Imperial and human inside the harem, I've accepted these mirror images of myself without questioning it too much. I tell myself that I'm less critical of my behavior because I'm leaving. I tell myself that if I were staying, I'd fight more for my independence.

But I know in my heart I don't know how I'd really feel if I didn't have a greater purpose here. The luxury and the back and forth with sentient and non-sentient roles has even muddled my mission. I'm not as determined as I was when I first arrived. And some days I even forget I do have a mission. But it's an easy thing to do. The women in the harem don't really want to be rescued. They've even said that if Gael the Returner were to come and open the harem gates they'd refuse to leave. So it makes me wonder what I'm doing here? These women don't want to be saved.

Many of the human women talk about their previous lives on Earth and some of them don't miss Earth at all. They tell me I was lucky to be taken so young. I retort with the movies and books I watched growing up but they tell me it's all fantasy, that for most women on Earth being a pet in Kamos's harem is better. *But that can't be true, can it?*

The longer I stay in the harem, the more I question myself and my promise to Gael. It's so peaceful here and the only decisions I have to make are what to eat and who to spend my day with if not summoned by Kamos.

Except nudging always in my mind is the term, 'Stockholm Syndrome.' I remember Gael mentioning it to me. And I think I may have it, but I don't think it's necessarily a bad thing to have when I'm safe, sound, and warm behind the harem gates.

A loud crash rips away my serenity. I hear more commotion and then loud voices. Ava is yelling which is very unusual. I jump out of bed. Rae and I rush out to the main common area where the head guard is trying to take Ava's daughter, Mei, but Ava won't let go of the little girl.

"No, she's not ready to go! She needs me. She's so young."

"She's of age. She'll be well looked after," the head guard is saying emphatically. "She doesn't need her human mother anymore."

"I'm her only mother," Ava cries frantically. "Don't take her from me! Just one last day! Please!"

"You knew this day was coming, Ava. You know how this all works. Say goodbye to Mei. She'll have a good life.."

Two more guards come to hold Ava back as a crying child is carried out screaming wildly, "Mommy! Mommy! Don't let them take me from you! Mommy! Mommy! No! Mommy!"

Ava is fighting against the guards who hold her. "Mei! Mei! Mommy loves you! Mei!!!" The guards finally let go of Ava when the head guard has left the harem. Ava cries on her knees. "My Mei. They took my baby. My Mei. She's gone."

It's difficult not to be affected by this. I was only a little older when I was taken from my own mother. I rush over to Ava but she throws me off. "Stay away from me! I just want Mei," she screams and begins sobbing again. Her whole body quaking with her sorrow. "My Mei."

I realize that I was not only looking to comfort Ava, but myself too, and I feel guilty for being so selfish. I watch with tears in my own eyes while Ava collapses on her side and howls primitively with heartbreak. I can do nothing for her. For all the luxury these women talk about, I think this emotional price is too high. And maybe they have such bad Stockholm Syndrome, they don't realize that the price of their captivity is too high. Or am I weak? Is this how life is for Imperial and humans and I'm the weak one? It doesn't matter because I'll never be able to see this from any different angle than my own and I condemn this.

I look around. Coco is nowhere to be seen. Not surprising. She doesn't want to witness this truth. She will be the one on the floor in five years, crying uncontrollably as her child is ripped from her arms.

I touch Ava's shoulder and say, "I am so sorry for you."

Ava, of course, doesn't even feel my hand or hear my words. It doesn't matter. I had to say something.

Rae and I return to my rooms.

"Where is the child going?"

"I don't know."

"If you could guess."

"Lora it's a nearby city. She'll be raised by Imperials now."

"Then what?"

"Maybe she'll become a servant like me," Rae says sadly. "Maybe worse."

I hug Rae and she hugs me back. “How are we all caught in this? Where are the goddesses now?” I asked that rhetorically.

“We are in the darkness,” Rae responds. “Born and raised in the darkness.”

My only response is silently to myself to do my duty to Gael and save as many people as possible. Any feelings I had that living in this harem was better than being free just vanished and will never be revisited. I turn my ring from Gael and focus again on trying to find that teleportation suit. What have I been doing wasting my time with frivolities, sex and gossip?

Chapter 19

Kamos

"Bring Lara here," I tell my young officer. Now that she's passed her language test her true training can begin. Humans are programable and I need to reprogram Lara. She's used to tentacles and now she needs to get used to pricks.

Lara is brought in on her silver leash. She has her chosen whip in her mouth and is wearing an appropriate pet outfit and not one owned by my previous alpha number two. Her breasts are well displayed and her nipples taut from being pulled on her leash.

"What took so long?"

"A lot of the men wanted to stroke her as we passed them in the corridors. Everyone loves a new pet."

I walk over to Lara and take her leash walking her to the center of the room. I stroke the fur between her legs. "And was she compliant? I'm sure she was," I answer my own question judging by the wetness I feel. Most humans are sex obsessed so they love the attention of the opposite sex which makes them good pets to have around for the morale of my crew. I dismiss my young officer. Then I instruct Lara,

"Open your legs wider for me." She does as I say. I rub her clit vigorously.

"Do you like this?"

She can't answer me because her whip is still in her mouth. I wipe some of her salvia off her chin. Then remove the whip from her mouth. It's a small whip.

"Yes Master," she replies breathlessly.

Then I purposely bring her close to orgasm and stop.

She makes a small whimper.

This is exactly what I want. It's such a pleasure to train new human pets. "Stay," I tell her and then I retrieve one of my favorite leather whips much larger than the one she brought. I show it to her. "Do you know what this is for?"

"Yes, Master."

"Did Lord Juo punish you?"

"No, Master."

"You were never a naughty human? I find that difficult to believe, but then again what do the Uru know of human females?" I run the whip between her legs, the leather becoming shiny with her desire. I'm purposely tempting her and she responds by moving forward on the whip. "Lara, to be a good pet you must learn control. Only a grey hand is allowed to bring you pleasure."

I can see in her green eyes that she's confused. I'm not surprised. Most humans don't have the intellect to understand or remember complex ideas. I put my hands on her petite hips. "Bend over."

Lara bends over and in her tight pet outfit, her backside is even more pronounced with the fabric framing her naked rear. I run my hands over both her cheeks. They're so pale. "I'm going to enjoy this."

There's nothing more erotic than watching a human's pink skin go even redder. "I can't believe Lord Juo wasted so many years painting you gold."

She begins to speak, but I whip her hard.

"Don't defend your previous master or speak unless I ask you a question." I whip her hard with the leather whip across the middle of her backside and my prick becomes aroused just as her pale skin turns red. "Blood is flowing for both of us. I want you to count how many lashes I give you and if you're a good pet, you'll be rewarded." I whip her again.

"One. Thank you, Master."

I rub one of her butt cheeks with my free hand. "Good girl." Then I whip her again.

"Two. Thank you, Master."

I don't stop. I continue to whip her and she continues to count although at number seven she lets out another moan. I know I'm pushing her to her limit. I pause and rub the whip between her legs. She's so close to orgasm. I can feel her body tense with the expectation of it. "You're in pain but your body also likes it. Do you want to orgasm?"

"Yes Master. Please rub your grey hand there."

"Of course you want to. But I won't allow it until I deem you've earned it. Understand?"

"Yes Master."

I lash her again and she counts always remembering to say, 'Thank you, Master.' This pleases me, she's so much further ahead than most new pets, but then again most of my new pets come directly from Earth. When she reaches ten lashes, I tell her, "Turn around and get on your knees. You've made me so aroused with your pale skin, you must relieve me before dinner."

Lara gets to her knees and takes down my trousers. Then she sucks on my dick so expertly it's difficult not to come right away. I knew Lara sucking on all those tentacles would make her good for something. I put my hands in her hair and push her further onto my dick. I feel myself hitting the back of her throat and I just continue guiding her head back and forth. Right before I come, I pull back and hold my prick to her lips. "Lap it up," I say and watch her lick at my come as it shoots out onto her lips and face. "Use your fingers to put it in your mouth."

Lara uses her pink tongue and pale fingers to scoop the hot liquid into her mouth.

I touch her between her legs. Her fur is dripping with human desire. "Be a good pet and you'll get what you want. Now, on your hands and knees go sit on the bed in the corner. Do not touch yourself or you won't get your reward." I watch her as she gets on her hands and knees and lays on her small human bed. I walk over and smack her backside, "Sit up."

She, of course, doesn't want to but I make her. I want her to feel her backside burning.

Soon my senior officers arrive. I usher Lara by her leash and my officers into my private dining room. I tell my best men, "Although I'm not ready to share her yet, I wanted to give you all a taste of my newest pet or rather *her* a taste of *you*."

My men are pleased by this and sit down in their assigned seats by rank.

I tell Lara, "Go under the table and swallow everything every man has for you. Start at this end."

Lara looks at me bewildered.

I push her to her knees and then under the table. "Suck every man's prick until he releases his hot liquid into your mouth," I tell her as plainly as I can. Lara is clever for a human, but she's still a human and can only understand so much. I watch her approach my first officer under the table. He undoes his trousers for her and she puts her mouth on him. I'm relieved I don't have to tell her again. Now the rest of us can eat and drink. I motion to my server to pour the wine.

"Oh, her hot human mouth is divine," my first officer says as Lara has her mouth over him. He puts his hands down to direct her and then groans as he comes into her mouth. He looks under the table at her mouth enveloping him and says, "Humans are so sexual it's unbelievable. Look how happy she is."

"We must taste so much better than tentacled Uru males."

"If she could understand how incredibly her life is now, she'd thank you for saving her."

"Humans can't think such complex thoughts."

"Kamos, she's rubbing herself against my shoe," my second officer informs me.

I look under the table and sure enough, Lara has her legs spread wide using his dirty shoe to pleasure herself. I should correct her behavior but I don't want to ruin the dinner. "Make her lick it clean after she finishes."

When Lara has swallowed every one of my officers' semen, and licked a lot of the men's shoes clean where she humped them, she obediently comes and sits by my side on the floor. I bring her up into my lap and fondle her breasts while my men and I continue to talk. She's so wet, her wanton desire is dripping onto my trousers. I point it out to my men and we all laugh. It's adorable how humans are. I know my men want to watch her orgasm here at the table, but I want to save her for myself.

When dinner is over I put Lara on the floor and tell her to go back to her pet bed in my room. When she doesn't go immediately, I think this is because she wants more sexual favors from my officers.

Humans are like that. They'll do anything for sex. I smack her behind. "Go."

My senior officers laugh as Lara goes on her hands and knees back to my bedroom, her leash dragging between her legs.

Once my officers have left, I return to my bedroom. "Lara, come here."

She comes to me on her hands and knees. I'm glad to see this, it means she's learning.

I pick her up and carry her to my bed. Once there I remove her clothing and my own. I think about her mostly good behavior tonight, "You're learning fast so now you'll get what you want." I use my fingers and rub her clit. It only takes a few minutes before she's writhing before me with pleasure. "Yes that's a good human pet. Come for me now. There we go. That's such a good girl. Look at all of this," I show her my wet fingers. "You're finally ready for me."

I get on top of her on the bed. "Put your hands above your head." I don't want her touching me when my mind is elsewhere, not until I trust her. Once her hands are in place, I have my bed clamp them down by the wrists so she can't move. Then I position myself between her legs. Her furry wet sex feels so good next to my hard prick. When I'm ready, I slowly push in. She moans. Of course she does. I pinch one of her nipples and then grab her leash as I begin moving in and out of her tight hole. *Goddesses she feels so good.* I thrust in and out of her quickly. Her ample breasts swaying vigorously with my movements despite me holding her leash up. After I've pounded into her so hard, I come, and then watch as my hot liquid trickles out, as her human hole is so small. I push some of my come back in with my fingers, then run more excess through her blonde fur. "You like that don't you? Another time, I'll have my men give you a hot semen shower." I promise her, I know human pets love that kind of attention. I lay on my side, one hand still between her legs and decide that

I'll keep Lara with me tonight. She's not trained to be an Imperial pet, per se, but she's still a very well-trained pet and I like having her next to me as I sleep.

Chapter 20

Lara

(Four Months Later)

Rae comes into the public baths where I'm relaxing with some of the other women from the harem. I know immediately she wants something by the look on her face.

"Kamos has asked for you."

I know this isn't something to rejoice over. Kamos's palace is run in a very predictable manner and he never 'plays with his pets' during these hours of the day.

"Come," she offers her hand to help me out of the water. "I'll help you prepare."

Rae escorts me back to my rooms and I dress in one of my finest pet outfits. It's like putting on a costume to perform a role. Rae slips the pink fabric over my head and I feel it caress my body as it falls to the floor. Long silver earrings are put in my ears and I watch in the mirror as she attaches my ornate silver leash to jeweled rings through my nipples.

Then she touches up my makeup. Pink blush and lipstick to emphasize what Imperials like about me the most, the way my pale cheeks flush with blood when I'm excited. *One man's trash is another's treasure* I think as I was always painted gold on the other side of the galaxy so those aliens wouldn't have to witness the consequences of my pale skin, which they found repulsive.

When I'm ready, I'm escorted out the locked ornamental gates of the harem across the palace. After walking for about ten minutes I realize I'm not being led to Kamos's private chambers. I want to ask where I'm being taken but I know better than to act like I'm sentient outside the harem. I'd give myself more of Hela's drug but it was removed from my arm during my last medical check.

When I'm led into Kamos's official waiting room for an audience I begin to become very concerned. Everyone waiting stares at me and I wonder why I'm here. *Have I been found out? Am I to be publicly executed?*

Chapter 21

Kamos and Lara

{Duet+Rae+First Minister}

l. Rae leads me in to Kamos's official receiving room. We bow when we reach Kamos and his guards at the other end of the large room. Looking around I've never seen such wealth on display nor so many impressive Imperial men in my life. The room is quiet with all eyes on me. I make eye contact with Kamos trying to read him, but his face reveals nothing. *Has he figured out that I've been reading his messages while he sleeps when I stay the night in his room?*

k. "Lara from Earth, then from Lord Juo and now mine," I say looking at my adorable pet. She's obedient and says nothing. "It wasn't mentioned in your provenance from Gala that you spent a week at the Fertility Goddess's Temple or time with Gael the Returner before you ended up in Gala. It says on this IGC report from the sex temple you married Gael. But this can't be true. Speak now and explain." Lara begins to explain herself in her seductively accented Imperial. It's difficult for me to believe she married Gael the Returner for anything but a Uru nun's cruel joke on her. Lara's mine now and I'm happy to have saved her from a half-life in the galaxy.

l. I know if I say one thing incorrectly, I will be found out so I choose my words carefully. "I was kept at the horrible Fertility Temple as a ward of the sadistic nuns. They beat me and told me that I'd die with an alien rutting inside of me. When Gael the Returner came, the nuns were disappointed I wouldn't die the way they wanted me to. They were upset about the UCs they wouldn't make by selling a video of an Agnorrian or Uru male's tentacled penis slowly poisoning me from inside as it rotted in my vagina. So they made Gael marry me if he wanted me so badly so then at least I would be off their hands."

k. "And then?"

l. "Gael the Returner gave me my freedom. He said he didn't keep pets. I pleaded with him to keep me." I touch my exposed breasts and the men in the receiving room murmur. "I showed him how pleasing I could be, but he refused me." I channel all the women's thoughts I've been surrounded by in the harem to make myself more convincing. "But Gael refused and the UCs he gave me ran out very quickly as I didn't know how to live. I don't want to be free in the galaxy. I'm used to being cared for. I'm an indoor human. So I allowed myself to be sold at Gala for a new master."

k. "It's as I thought, you're not a stupid pet. However I'll have to keep you very safe from now on. Even if your marriage to Gael wasn't real to you, he won't annul it and it's real to the IGC. Which means the IGC is after you." I watch Lara's face expression to see if she knows what this is about. She seems genuinely confused. "You see, my sweet little pet, Gael the Returner's wife, you are legally responsible for all of his crimes. That's the matriarchy for you."

l. I hear Kamos's words and my world begins to spin. I think I'm going to faint. Out of the corner of my eye I see Kamos jump up and run to me. The next thing I know I'm looking up at familiar grey faces.

r. "It's the pregnancy I'm sure. She was healthy just a moment ago."

l. It's not the pregnancy. It's the knowledge that I'm responsible for Gael's crimes and that he won't annul the marriage. *Is our marriage real to him? Or does he plan on making me take the blame for all of his crimes? Why is Kamos in touch with Gael again? Have I been duped?*

k. "Lara, I won't let the IGC have you." I say to her, then to Rae, "Take her to the medical center to make sure she really is fine." I watch as Rae and my guards carry Lara away. As soon as they have left my first minister addresses me.

fm."She could be lying."

k. "To what end? Gael wouldn't be able to fully protect her from the IGC and it wouldn't have been difficult for her to find out that I'm one of the only people who could offer her a good life and IGC protection on this side of the galaxy. I think Coco is jealous of her and as for Gael well, it's believable that he would've done that to free her. Of course he would have."

fm."It seems too convenient that she was brought to Gala on the same day you were buying though."

k. I hold up my hand. "It was a coincidence or as I'd like to see it, good fortune. I'll hear no more of this. If she were a spy she wouldn't be such an eager pet and she would've definitely learned better Imperial before coming here. She's been not only compliant but agreeable."

fm."And she's carrying your child."

k. "That's only a testament to her wanting to make a permanent home here," I say. Since Lara passed the language test my cultural minister devised for her, I've rewarded her by having her sleep in my rooms at least a few times a week to retrain her in what men like on this side of the galaxy. She's become one of my favorite pets and I won't give her up because my first minister has his doubts. "You're being overly cautious about a harmless human pet."

Chapter 22

Lara

In the medical center, the doctor insists on running a complete scan. Rae and the guards wait by my side. No one is talking except the doctor to his assistant. "The pregnancy looks good."

After another ten minutes the doctor says to Rae, "You must keep her calm."

"I will."

"You may go."

Rae searches my eyes. "Can you walk?"

"Yes," I say, taking her arm for support. The guards continue to follow us all the way back to the ornate gates of the harem. Once there, I want to go speak with Coco. She knows more about the galaxy and Gael than anyone else. But when I try to walk away from Rae she holds me back.

"You must rest."

"I want to see Coco."

"You can't she's having her baby soon. She's been taken away to the birthing place."

"Where's that?"

"Not here."

"When will she be back?"

"She'll return when she and the baby are healthy."

I didn't like the sound of that. I obediently follow Rae into my room and lay down on my bed. I stare at the carved wood pattern in the window. It's a flower of life pattern. I touch my abdomen and wonder if Gael has abandoned me.

In the middle of the night a burning sensation on my finger wakes me up. It takes me a minute to realize that it's the lovers' ring. I frantically try to remember today's date. It's the 5th day of the week. The 5th day! I sit up with anticipation. It must have been my passing out in Kamos's reception room that sent the signal. Now I must decide. *Is my mission real or does Gael only want me to steal this and then go on trial for all of his crimes with the IGC?*

I look around my semi dark room. It's so peaceful. Rae is sleeping in the corner and a slight breeze is coming in through the window. This isn't a bad situation. I absently put a hand to my stomach again and remember that it's not just me anymore. I'm pregnant with Kamos's child. *Can I allow this child to be born into this?*

If it's a girl she most certainly will be. She'll be taken away just like Ava's little girl. And then it'll be my turn to play the part of Ava. And I never want to experience that. No matter if this child is grey or pale-pink like me, I know if it's born, I'll love it, and then if it's taken from me, I will lose all grip on reality. I've never experienced love except maybe with Gael, but after seeing Ava and Mei together, I think a mother's love is stronger than any other bond. And what's happened has broken Ava and I don't know if she'll ever recover. I don't want to do that to myself without a fight.

I quietly move, always keeping my eyes on Rae. To send the clearest signal back to Gael I need to masturbate. These are lovers' rings after all. But I don't want to do that in my bed. First, because it's forbidden for me to touch myself and second, I worry I'll wake Rae up. As silently as I can, I walk into the bathroom which is far from the bedroom and close the door. I lean up against the stone wall and push my nightdress up around my hips. I begin touching myself before I think too much about this plan. Although my feelings are mixed I know that on the whole, I want to leave more than I want to stay. Even though, all of this, this illusion of peacefulness and luxury is a very alluring drug and, had I never experienced life on the outside, I might have stayed here never tasting freedom and assuming this is the best life had to offer.

A few minutes after I've orgasmed, I get the same response from Gael. Now he waits. All I need to do is figure out a way out of the harem and to the armory where I can steal the teleportation suit. I know where it is. I also know the head guard has a master key to everywhere in the palace including the armory.

It didn't take me long to figure out Kamos's codes while I stayed in his bedroom. He often would use his code right in front of me. So as far as I'm concerned I didn't even have to steal it. He basically told it to me. With his code I could look at everything including what was stored in the armory and who had master keys.

The head guard of the harem was another situation altogether. She is a straightforward large woman who doesn't seem to have a weakness. She knows better than Kamos than to let her guard down around humans. I don't want to have to hurt anyone in my escape but there might be no other way. I've seen a lot of violence in my life and I have had to kill before. I hope that I won't have to do it again.

It's peaceful tonight. *Maybe I should go now?* Inspiration takes over and I take a carving knife from my small dining room. Then I go back to the bedroom. Rae is still asleep which I'm grateful for. I don't want to have to kill her. I quietly slip out my front door and tiptoe through the harem to the head guard's room.

I stand in front of it and of course it's locked for the night. With shaky hands I ring the bell. I hold the knife innocently behind my back as I wait.

She answers. None of her other guards are in sight. "Lara?"

I don't wait. I rush her and plunge the knife into her side. I stab her again and again. Red blood is going everywhere. She doesn't' even scream she just has a very surprised look on her face. She didn't even have time to throw me off. Adrenaline is pumping through me. I'm covered in blood, but the head guard seems dead. I step over her body, drag her in and then close her door. Just in case, I tie her hands up. Then I quickly run into her bathroom and wash all the blood off of me. I contemplate putting on one of her dresses, but I think that will only raise more suspicion. I take her master key and a gun. Then, I run, naked, closing her door behind me. As far as I know I've managed to do that without an alarm sounding, but I know it'll sound soon. The medical system counts heartbeats in the compound every 20 minutes. If I'm lucky I have 20 minutes from now. If I'm unlucky, only a few minutes or less. I run as fast as I can. My bare feet silently hitting the stone. I slow when I reach the ornate harem gates. I eye the guards who seem very relaxed but they aren't sleeping.

I saunter up to them. "Good evening. Kamos has requested I see him."

"Now?"

"Yes."

"Where's your servant?"

"She's ill and the head guard said for me to just go."

They don't look convinced.

I push out my stomach more than it really is. "I'm already pregnant with Kamos's child and the IGC has a bounty out for me. Trust me I'm not going anywhere." News travels fast through the palace so I've no doubt everyone here knows I'm married to Gael and now responsible for all of his crimes.

"What he did to you is terrible," one of the guards laments as the other opens the gate.

"To use a helpless human woman like that," the other guard says and shakes his head.

"Thankfully Kamos rescued me and I'm safe with Imperials like you protecting me," I say as I slowly walk away. I'm glad the guards didn't notice what was in my hands, how much I was sweating, or could hear my heartbeat which seems almost deafening in my ears. They like most of the guards were just looking at my naked female body as I walked past.

As soon as I'm far enough away not to cause suspicion, I begin to run again. I've never been to the armory but I have a good idea where it is. I run through the deserted corridors until I see more guards. I stop running when I reach them.

"Oh I'm so glad you're here, I'm lost," I say.

They immediately are sympathetic and begin to try and help. I take out the head guard's gun from behind my back and shoot them both quickly multiple times. They never even drew their weapons they thought I was so helpless they were momentarily stunned by a human with a gun. *I can't believe they don't see me as a threat even when I'm armed.* Then, I run into what I think is the armory. It looks like it. But it's much bigger than I thought it'd be and confusing. After a few minutes I feel like I'm walking in circles.

"Come on. How do I find this thing?" I ask myself. Then I spot a tablet hanging on a wall. I have no idea how I missed it before. I put in Kamos's code and search the device. I'm led right to the teleportation device.

It looks like a plain black suit with a helmet. *This can't be it. How can I get away and through the forcefield with this?*

I put the suit on over my naked body and then put on the helmet. Nothing is working and I can hear my heart beating in my ears. *Am I going to die?* I can't remember how to turn this on.

I hear the sound of the alarm. They know what I've done. It's now or never. I begin frantically rubbing my hands up and down the outside of the suit and then I remember the controls are on the back of the helmet. I press them and then find the coordinates in the visor in front of my face. I'm so scared I can hardly read the Imperial hieroglyphs I memorized with Gael.

I hesitate before I hit initiate. I may die. This is a prototype. Maybe it's not too late. *Would Kamos forgive me if I stayed?* I consider this for half a second.

No, what's wrong with me? I can't stay. I want my freedom even if I die trying.

I hear the guards enter the armory yelling for me. "Lara, where are you? You've been a naughty little pet! Come out come out wherever you are. You must be punished you devilish little human."

I take a deep breath and punch the engage button.

Pooooofffff. My molecules are separating into a thousand pieces and there's nothing. I'm weightless. There's nothing but black. Then nothing but light. Suddenly I take a deep breath and I can feel my heartbeat again. My eyes flicker and I open my eyes. I'm somewhere. I don't see anyone though. I'm alone in a modern room.

The helmet only tells me I've arrived.

My bracelet on my left wrist begins to beep and I scramble to try to get it off, but it's too late it's injected me with poison. I forgot about this. I can't die now.

I check the door. I'm locked in.

I'm trapped and I'm going to die from poison unless Kamos's men come for me and give me the antidote. *How could I be so stupid?*

While trying to figure out a way out of the room, one side of the room lights up with Kamos's face. "Lara I'm disappointed that my first minister was correct. Did you really think I'd keep a teleportation suit open for anyone? Of course it was programmed to go to a holding cell."

Before I can answer him, the door breaks down and Gael is there. He looks like a dream he's so handsome dressed in black armor. He whips out a syringe and says, "It's the antidote, come here." I run into his arms but he only embraces me for a second before plunging the medicine into my arm. "We're in the middle of a bit of a skirmish. Stand behind me."

But suddenly the shooting stops and Kamos addresses Gael. "Gael the Returner, is she really your wife?"

I feel like Kamos has just asked the one question in the entire universe that I really want to know too. And it's deadly silent as we wait for an answer.

"Lara from Earth is my legal wife."

Kamos is so still on the screen I think the connection has frozen but then he says, "If you two would rather sacrifice yourselves and risk your own happiness for human strangers than you must be rewarded. The goddesses will decide your fate."

"What?" I say trying to understand what Kamos meant, but Gael doesn't say anything. Instead he grabs the helmet to the teleportation suit and my hand and we run. It reminds me of when he ran with me trying to escape the Fertility Goddess's Temple. "I hope this time we make it out."

As we approach some Terra Ka members Gael begins shouting at them. "We have a seven second reprieve! Go! Go! Go! We have the suit! Go!" His men don't hesitate and begin running. It's not long before we enter his stealth transport and we're on our way back to the *Sisu.* A couple shots are fired at us but miss the cloaked transport.

I can't believe this is real. *Did I really escape? Or am I dead without my flash of memories?* I look around at the men in the transport. I recognize most of them and if this were a dream I don't think I could conjure up these faces some of which I only saw a few times. I look back through the transport window, "What was that place?"

"Kamos's own private prison," one of the Terra Ka men explains. "We were informed the suit was programmed to go there no matter what coordinates were entered."

"But how did we get away? What did Kamos mean when he said the goddesses would decide our fate?"

"That we had seven seconds before he killed us. It's from an Imperial myth about lovers who sacrificed themselves for the greater good."

"Is that why he's not in pursuit now?"

"No. He's not prepared now, but he knows who's taken his suit. He won't give up that easily."

"He'll torture and kill me. I killed some people when I escaped," I confess.

"Don't worry," Seo says from across the transport. "You're probably going to die a free woman. Now if you don't mind please hand me the suit. I'm going to reprogram it so we can use it right away. We've men waiting to free everyone from an Imperial Pet Compound right now. We're going to save hundreds all thanks to you. And they'll be returned to Earth before their window of opportunity closes. Well done, Lara."

I want to accept his praise but it bounces off of me. I don't know why. Perhaps because of the lives I took in my pursuit of the suit or all the sexual things I did. So I say nothing but I take off the suit in the cramped quarters of the transport. What I didn't expect is for all the Imperial men to look the other way as I did it. It is like night and day with how these Imperials think of me as opposed to those in Kamos's palace. I hand Seo the suit and sit back down naked, my skin sticking against the seat. Gael immediately takes off his jacket and hands it to me. It's so large it falls down to my thighs. Then I ask, "What's that supposed to mean? 'I'll die a free woman.'"

Gael answers me in English, "The IGC is after you for my crimes. The nuns from the Fertility Temple logged our marriage and Kamos has been hit with numerous fines for buying a free citizen at Gala. It's made a lot of headlines. It proves that humans are actually free and the IGC is going to begin enforcing the law to a certain degree. Lara, you're the first human to be recognized as a galactic citizen."

I let those words sink in. "Say that last part again."

Gael puts his hand over mine. "You're the first human to be recognized as a free galactic citizen. Not only did you steal the teleportation suit you've begun a real movement. The IGC has become fractured with those who want to uphold the law and those who want to continue to allow human trafficking. This is better than we ever hoped all because you misunderstood the Uru phrase of 'choosing' someone."

I was happy until his last sentence brought me down a bit. I give him a fake half smile. Of course I'm more than pleased with this outcome but the truth is right now all I want is Gael to tell me he loves me. I catch his gaze and wait. He doesn't say anything so I say, "So Kamos wasn't lying?"

"What did he say?"

"Just that I was responsible for your crimes because I'm your wife."

"You are. The IGC is a matriarchy. The idea is that no woman would marry a criminal if she were responsible for his crimes as well."

I push Gael out of frustration. "Why didn't you tell me?"

"Would it had made a difference? Would you have stayed at the sex temple or would you have stayed with Kamos?"

I stamp on his foot with my own to do something because he's right. I would have made the exact same choices. But more than anything I want him to take me into his arms and say he wanted to marry me too.

By the time we reach the *Sisu*, I walk off and try to walk to what used to be my room. I just want to be alone to think about everything.

Gael grabs my arm. "Where are you going?"

"To be alone."

"You've got to see Hela."

Gael doesn't let go of my arm as he escorts me to the doctor. Many people offer their congratulations as we walk through the hallways. I can barely keep the tears from my eyes. My emotions are everywhere right now and I don't know how to get them in check.

When we walk into the medical center Hela begins to greet us but then her face loses all its warmth. "Come here Lara. Gael, go somewhere else. This is a matter for women only."

When Hela and I are alone the first thing she does is put her hands on my bare arms. Immediately I begin to feel better and more in control. "What are you doing?"

"I'm easing some of your adrenaline. You're all worked up."

"For good reason. I killed some people. I'm not a killer."

"Everyone is capable of killing if they need to be. I can erase those memories right now. Do you want me to?"

I consider her offer. "No. I need to know what I did."

"You don't need to know the details."

I think about this again. "No I need it all or else I'll always wonder. At least this way I know why."

Hela nods and then uses a device to cut off my bracelet and remove the tracking chip from my arm. "Now there's the question of this pregnancy. Did you tell anyone in the rescue party?"

"No. But they all saw me naked. This is Gael's jacket."

"We can tell them you were bloated. Now what do you want to do?"

"What do you mean?" I meet her grey eyes.

"Don't tell me you want to keep it?"

"It's half mine."

"Who's the other half?"

"Kamos," I say as if I'm ashamed, but I was his pet. I was playing a part. I wasn't cheating on Gael. Gael sent me there.

"And you still want to keep it?"

I feel like a child asking for permission. "Yes, I want to keep it. How can you ask me that? Most of you here are half human. What if your mothers had aborted you?" I know I'm raising my voice I just can't help it. I feel the ring on my finger freezing and as soon as I notice it Gael has returned, his face in anguish.

Hela says, "She's perfectly healthy, but she should rest."

"I'm not a pet!" I yell. "I'm standing right here."

Hela looks me in the eyes. "I'm sorry Lara. Please go and rest. You are perfectly healthy."

Chapter 23

Gael and Lara

{Duet}

l. I don't say anything but storm out of the medical center. I start making my way to where my quarters used to be but Gael stops me.

g. "Come, take my quarters. I will sleep elsewhere."

l. "No."

g. "Please."

l. "No. I just want to be in my own space."

g. "You can't be in the room you had before. It's occupied. We're completely full. And now that this is done I thought..."

l. "You thought what?"

g. "Lara, you are my wife."

l. "You thought that we were going to have sex? Just pretend nothing happened between us leaving the Fertility Goddess's Temple and now?" I look at him in disbelief. "Has everyone lost their minds? Do you know what I had to do in Kamos's palace? Do you have any idea how close I was to staying? Oh and also, you could have told me you and Coco were lovers? That was a nasty surprise."

g. I motion with my hand for her to enter my quarters. "Let's at least discuss this in private."

l. Inside I'm too angry to sit down so we both stand in his sitting room. "I'm waiting for you to explain yourself."

g. "Coco and I had sex a few times. It was mostly physical and more than a year before I met you. It meant very little to either of us which is why it wasn't important to mention."

l. "You and I didn't have a deep emotional connection before we married and had sex," I point out. "Yet you treat me differently. How can that be?"

g. "Because *you* are different. You've always been different. Sex is just touching another body for momentary physical desire. But I swear I have only ever made love to you. It was different even that first time. We have a deep connection and I know you feel it too."

l. "But then why didn't you touch me when we came onboard the *Sisu*? I was practically begging for any kind of physical connection then."

g. "I wanted to, but how could I do that with what I was asking you to do?"

l. "But now you think..."

g. "Lara, no I didn't think you were just going to jump in bed with me. But I wanted you to have my room at the very least."

l. "Are you saying you really want to be married? Is that why you didn't annul it? Not to make me stand trial?"

g. "I swear to you, I will kill myself before I let the IGC take you for my crimes. And just so you know, if I'm dead you're off the hook." I take out my gun and hand it to her. "Shoot me now and you're free of me and my crimes."

l. I begin to cry.

g. Seeing Lara like this is overwhelming. I take my gun back before she hurts herself or me and then I take her into my arms slowly. She doesn't resist. I stroke her hair. "I'm so sorry."

l. "I thought all this time you didn't want me. I thought you were only using me and that you hadn't even been honest about why and that you were going to leave me with Kamos."

g. "No that would've never happened. I would've gotten you out."

l. I look up at him. "How?"

g. "I've not been completely honest with you Lara. I have a connection to Kamos."

l. "I know I overheard Kamos say he bought some very young children and sent them to you to return to Earth. That you'd both profit from it."

g. "Yes, we are two sides of the same coin. We both are criminals in the galaxy. I break the laws by abducting humans and returning them to Earth. He breaks the laws by providing Imperials with every illegal thing they want including humans. But we are more than just business acquaintances. Our relationship is much closer."

l. "I'm not following. Did you used to work for Kamos?"

g. "No. It's closer than that. Lara, Kamos is my father."

l. "No! No! No!" I shake my head. "That's not possible. Why would you send me to be your father's sex pet? That's not right Gael. That's insane. How could you do that? No wonder you never wanted to touch me after our marriage at the Fertility Temple."

g. Lara tries to move away from me, but I hold her tight as she screams into my chest. "I'm sorry. I didn't want to make it any more difficult than it already was. I knew if you knew the truth and I acted selfishly and acted on my own desires to treat you as my true wife, which is what I always wanted, that you wouldn't go."

l. "You're right I wouldn't have. It's incestuous. It's wrong." I wipe my hands down my arms and step away from him.

g. "It's not like my father and I shared you at the same time. You're my wife. I'm never going to share you."

l. "But you have and now I'm pregnant with your father's child!"

g. I just thought she had gained weight from all the delicious food on offer at Kamos's palace when I saw her naked in the transport. "You're sure it's Kamos's?"

l. "I only had the kind of sex that makes you pregnant with your father while I was there. He was quite determined. How did you think I was able to get all the codes and steal the teleportation suit? I feel like vomiting." I walk towards the door.

g. "Where are you going? The toilet is over there."

l. "I'm going to the medical center to take something out of the equation."

g. "No. Don't abort her. She's my half-sibling and you're her mother."

l. My heart hurts a little when he uses the default feminine pronoun because the galaxy is a matriarchy. The truth is, I, of course, would want to have a daughter. "You want me to keep a child with you fathered by your own father?"

g. "Yes."

l. "And you don't find this whole situation incestuous?"

g. "We are keeping it in the family, but, Lara, all families are messy in the galaxy."

l. "And when this child asks who her father is?"

g. "Where would her curiosity come from unless someone told her? Who knows you are pregnant with Kamos's child?"

l. "Kamos. The whole palace. You and Hela. That's a lot of people."

g. "Kamos won't come for you if you're with me. He respects me as a worthy adversary. And he won't say anything because it'll make him look bad. There'll only be rumors."

l. Something's not right here. I take a deep breath and close my eyes. Then I ask, even though I don't know if I want to hear the answer, "Did Kamos give me to you as some kind of gift?"

g. "Why would you ask that?"

l. "How did you know the transporter suit would go there? How did you have the antidote to the poison bracelet? How could we escape from Kamos's private prison?"

g. "Inside information."

l. "From Kamos? I have to know Gael. Tell me."

g. "Once Kamos found out we were married he contacted me to discuss the situation. He at first thought it was as you said, but when I wouldn't annul the marriage it didn't take him long to figure out what was going on."

l. "And?"

g. "We came to an agreement."

l. "Did you buy me?"

g. "I'll not lie to you. UCs were exchanged but it wasn't that simple. Your freedom was also dependent upon you. If you could escape with the teleportation suit, showing your intelligence, desire to be free, and your commitment to me and humanity, Kamos swore he'd give us passage and wouldn't come after us. But he honestly didn't believe you'd try to escape. You played your pet part very well. He was completely smitten with your pet stupidity."

l. "How do you have a relationship with a man who actively is against everything you're trying to do with your life?"

g. "We don't have a relationship like you think. He's my father, but I was sent away from the palace when I was a boy. I didn't see him or my mother again until I was an adult. I hate him for what he did to my mother. But business is business and he's a criminal just like I am. As far as human pet owners go he's one of the better ones." I hold up my hand before she interjects. "That doesn't mean I condone it at all. Never forget my life's mission. But unfortunately the galaxy is not black and white. To do good things, sometimes I must do bad things. I must have relationships with bad people and never forget, the galaxy sees me as a criminal just as much as it does Kamos. And we both have politicians and IGC officers sympathetic to both of our causes."

l. I feel used. I take off the lovers' ring and throw it across the room. "Then why did your mother and Kamos have those?"

g. "My mother had those with another man she loved. The Imperial man who founded Terra Ka and a man that I admired greatly until his death. And he died repatriating humans."

l. Instantly, I feel guilty for throwing the ring. I quickly retrieve it. Placing it in Gael's hand I say, "I'm sorry."

g. "It's a lot to take in. You were kept by Lord Juo for so long and although you were abused, you were ignorant of the way slavery works on this side of the galaxy."

l. So many revelations are coming to me all at once, but I only have one question I want to know. "Are we really married? Or do you want to annul it? I don't want to be someone's pity prize. Nor do I want you taking me as your wife just to hold something over your father for leverage."

g. I lean down and cup her delicate face in my hands. "Lara, I love you. I'd do anything for you including sacrifice myself. You've proved to me that you'd do almost anything for me, including sacrifice yourself too. Now we have a baby that is a blood relation to both of us. We don't ever need to mention the circumstances of her conception. And trust me Kamos was going to see how that child looked and then decide her fate, just like he did mine and all my half-siblings. Kamos only misses the amount of UCs I paid him for you. Make no mistake, now I know you're pregnant I know what I was paying for."

l. I look directly into his green eyes. His sincerity is shocking. I want to believe in this fantasy but can I live with myself raising a child here knowing who his father really is? "If I were to leave? Return to Earth?"

g. "That's illegal and you know it."

l. "That doesn't stop you from going there illegally."

g. "To return humans according to IGC laws. You know that. You've been gone from Earth too long ever to return. The Empire monitors Earth and they'd remove you and then you'd be in the same if not worse situation than you're in now. The IGC would arrest you for my crimes and you would have to stand trial. They might let you off, but I don't know. A human has never been put on trial before. I think you understand what your choices are but you don't want to make a decision. But you must decide, Lara."

l. I don't want to be put on trial for Gael's crimes, but I don't want to kill him either. He does so much good for the galaxy and despite what he's done to me, I still love him. "If I stay, what happens when our child grows up?"

g. "What do you mean?"

l. "You wouldn't send her away. I haven't seen any children here."

g. "I would want you both to live at our base."

l. "Terra Ka has a base?"

g. "Of course we do."

l. "And our child can live there and be free?"

g. "As free as she can be. If she looks human that'll be an issue unless the IGC moves faster than expected. New laws about species being free takes generations to take hold in daily life. You have your freedom. I won't keep you with me if you don't want to stay. But I want you to stay, Lara. I love you. I love what you've done for Terra Ka, for me, but most importantly for humans in the galaxy. I'm sorry your freedom has come at such a high cost. I'm sorry you're now also responsible for my crimes and having my father's child. But I can offer you a slice of galactic freedom on the Terra Ka base as my human wife. Please say it's enough Lara."

l. I look up at Gael. I realize now that I was never going to be truly free. I feel so much disappointment I waver, but Gael catches my elbow and steadies me. I reflect that I'm freer than I was yesterday.

g. It's agony waiting for her decision. "I promise you can open and close all the doors as much as you want."

l. "I will never be truly free, will I?"

g. "The law says you are free, but how quickly society moves, I don't know. It might always be a fight. But our daughter will be freer than you. Be her steppingstone. And if she ever asks about her real father you can decide whether or not to tell her the truth, but know this, what you did by getting this teleportation suit will save countless other humans from suffering your fate. And inadvertently you're being sold at Gala has pushed the IGC to enforce the law that humans are free citizens. What you've done is nothing to be ashamed of and I'm proud of you Lara."

l. I'm struck by his words and finally his praise reaches my soul and I embrace it. I begin to cry a little. "I have to tell you something to get it off my chest. I don't want you to wonder about it later."

g. "There's *nothing* you have to tell me," I say. I know she wants to tell me about what she had to do at the palace. "What you had to do, it doesn't matter to me. I love you. That's what's important to me. What did you say before you left? 'What is sex but exchanging a little bit of body fluids and muscle contractions.'"

l. "That was before I knew what it'd be like with Imperial men, so physically close to humans. I want to let you know it was different... I was unprepared for how my body would react. How *I* would react emotionally..." Looking at him I don't know if I have the strength to tell him, but I must. "I wasn't raped," I say and wait for his response. For years I'd been owned by jealous males, so I expect Gael to be upset by this.

g. "Good."

l. I'm floored. Gael pulls me into his strong embrace and begins stroking my hair.

g. "Good," I say again. I'm relieved to know that she wasn't raped. I still carry the guilt of knowing how I was conceived. And it's awkward thinking about her and my father together and that I put her in that situation. "I'm sure it wasn't amazing all the time though. You did come back to me."

l. "Do you think that's why Coco stayed to be with your father?"

g. "I don't know."

l. "She told me she loved your father and that she also wanted to be a mother even if the time spent with her child would be fleeting. I'm guessing you didn't want that?"

g. "We never talked about it. But I couldn't offer her anything luxurious." I gesture around to my quarters. "I thought that might get you too. All those fine material things. I know things weren't easy for you at first on the *Sisu*."

l. I look away. I'm ashamed that I enjoyed being pampered in the harem. Humiliated that I enjoyed my golden cage and that I even contemplated that life wasn't that bad being owned by Kamos. I'm uncomfortable that I had sex and became pregnant with his father's child. I never wanted that, but I never said 'no' either. "Gael had I known he was your father..."

g. "You would have never gone and you would have never been able to steal the teleportation suit. It's the only one of its kind and it'll allow us to get in and out of places to help without anyone knowing we have it."

l. "Kamos knows."

g. "True but he's not going to tell the authorities it exists explicitly. You did a great job. We'll record this in the Terra Ka legacy along with the note that your actions have put pressure on the IGC to ensure humans' rights by being the first human to be recognized as a free citizen. Buyers at Gala will be more concerned now because they're thinking, 'If Kamos can be caught then what about me?'"

l. I didn't expect those words to mean so much to me but suddenly they do. "You're going to record my actions?"

g. "Yes. For what our group is worth we record what we've done and what works so that others can learn and feel inspired."

l. "Can you write it as, 'Lara from Earth, Wife of Gael?'"

g. "I can, but..."

l. "I want to choose freedom wherever I can. I don't want anyone who owned me to tarnish the good I have done today." I touch my abdomen. "I don't want her to see my name as being owned by anyone in the Terra Ka records. Every place I went in the galaxy I had to name my owners and where I was sold. She'll be able to find that information anywhere. I want a record of me somewhere where I'm not owned."

g. "So does this mean you still *choose* me, Lara?"

l. I answer him in Uru which he can understand with his translator. "I *choose* you, Gael the Returner." Although I learned those words when I was owned by Lord Juo, they seem very fitting and authentic now. "I'm free and I choose you." Gael's lips touch mine. And it's as if he's kissing me for the first time again. I tremble. His lips send electricity through me and I put my hands in his black hair to pull him closer.

g. "I'm grateful, Lara," I say as I hold her tightly against me. I want her in ways I've never wanted any other woman. Nothing matters to me but Lara. I run my hands down her body. This body that I've thought about every day since I met her but haven't touched since that first day.

l. I've fantasized about being back with Gael ever since I left him. I want this more than ever now. But I've changed. When he first touched me he was the first man with hands like mine to do so. *Now how many grey hands have touched me?*

g. I pull back my kiss and search her green eyes for answers. When I don't find them I say, "I've thought about you every day since you left," and then add, "And even before that." I worry that she doesn't find me attractive anymore. That I don't add up to my father.

l. "Why do you want me now?"

g. "You're my wife." I run my hands up and down her small torso. "I've missed you. But you don't have to..." I move my hands back into my own space.

l. "I don't want you to think you have to."

g. I'm confused. *Why wouldn't she want me to touch her?* I stay silent while I try to figure this out. Our eyes never break contact. "Does my touch repel you because of my father?"

l. "No. No! How can you even suggest that?" I feel sick that that's where his mind went, but at least it gives me an opportunity to say how I feel which is less incestuous. "So many grey hands have touched me now. Pleasured me...." I trail off. *How can I continue?* "Am I still attractive to you?"

g. I take her into my arms and kiss the top of her head, then I rest my head on hers reveling in her being in my arms. "Lara, I sent you to Kamos's palace. I always wanted you back. I will always want you and you will always be mine, unless you don't want me. And if I'm being pedantic, I was your first man and that was also the day we married and you became mine forever."

l. I wrap my arms around his strong body and hold him close. How could I have ever thought that he wouldn't have wanted me? It's because *I* feel used. "It was all work for me in the palace. This isn't work. You are my pleasure, Gael." He squeezes me so tightly I feel like I might not be able to breathe.

g. "And you are mine, always." I kiss the top of her head, her forehead, her nose, her lips. My tongue enters her small mouth. "All of you is mine," I say in-between kisses. My mind is telling me not to say these things, but I'm on autopilot now and my emotions are running this show. There's no logic in what I want from her. No galactic manners or customs, just my primal instincts as a man. I begin kissing her neck as I run my hands through her long blonde hair. "And I will *never* share you again."

l. His touch is igniting a fire within my body I've not felt since I was last here. All my fears about only being attracted to Gael because he was the first humanoid man I'd ever been with melt away. "I never feel like this with anyone else. Only you. Your touch is the only man's that reaches my soul."

g. "So, not my father?" I had to ask. I have to get this out of my system so that I can move on too.

l. "Stop mentioning Kamos. Definitely not. You don't even look anything like him. He's a cruel and terrible man." Somewhere in my lustful mind I think this must have come from Coco leaving him for his father. Even though it's such a messed up situation. So interconnected but with two teams on opposite sides. The palace and Terra Ka. One place where I'm a pet and the other I'm a woman. Both had their charms. As Gael kisses down my body he stops at my nipple piercings and moves the silver rings back and forth.

g. "Do you want these out?" I don't want her to wear these. They are the sign of an Imperial woman or a human pet. I want neither for my human wife.

l. "I want them out. I'll never be led around with a leash connected to my nipples ever again."

g. I gently remove the jewelry from her nipples and throw them on the floor. They silently fall somewhere. I don't even care. Then I take each of her breasts in my hand and kiss her pink nipples softly. As if I'm kissing away the pain associated with how they were used. "These nipples will serve a greater purpose now." She doesn't say anything but just makes a little sound of pleasure. I make my way down to her stomach and lower abdomen. I see my father's brand there. I run my finger over it. I can't help but remember the same brand on my mother. And for a minute I allow myself to mourn her. *How can I not? But Lara's saved herself.*

l. "I want that removed."

g. "We can try," I tell her. "It's not a simple brand. But I've heard of Dulu who can remove it."

l. "Is it possible to alter? Make it a full circle or something? I don't want it on me."

g. I kiss her brand. "I'll make it a priority for Hela to figure out." Then I move further down her body. She's just as soft and stunning as I remember. I run my hands through the hair between her legs and she jumps as if no one has touched her but me in months.

l. Gael's touch is completely different than those of Kamos or any of his men. Gael caresses me like a man who's acquainted with my soul. Not just a nameless, non-sentient pet. His touch sends goosebumps up and down my body. "I've missed you so much," I say as his finger begins opening my sex up for him.

g. I kiss her hard on her nether lips, my tongue seeking out her clit, and pick her up. Her legs around my shoulders. I hold her against my face as I lick her clit. Her scent bewitches me and I bring her to orgasm while holding her. Then I carry her over to my bed, I lay her down, and strip off my clothing. All the while looking at her displayed on my bed, naked and wanting. I lay down next to her and kiss her again.

l. His kisses make all the difference. No one at the palace ever kissed me. Not even Kamos. He just used me. They all used me like a business transaction. I was given material goods for the obedient sex I provided. *It was work. This is passion. This is desire. This is real.* Gael's tongue in my mouth brings tears to my eyes.

g. I wipe the tears from her flushed cheeks with my thumbs. Then I kiss each one. "Are you here with me?"

l. "Yes. I'm crying because I'm *really* here. I was dead for most of my life with Lord Juo. My first breath of life in the galaxy was when you touched me in the temple. But I was submerged again at Kamos's palace. So many people have touched me, and I felt nothing but the physical sensation. I was only a puppet and anyone could pull my strings and make my body perform. But when you touch me, Gael, I feel like I'm living, not just going through the motions of existing and no one is pulling my strings but me. I can't explain how moving that is for me to feel this."

g. I run my finger over her bottom lip. "I feel the same when I'm with you. You're touch ignites my heart. I've never been with anyone who makes me feel this way." I lean down and kiss her and as I do, I slowly position myself at her entrance. She spreads her legs wider for me and I enter her fully on my first thrust. I look down at her below me. "You are my wife, Lara, my real wife. I'm sorry you ever doubted that. I never doubted you. I love you." I say as I withdraw and then thrust into her again. Her breasts move with my rhythm and her hands feel good on my back. "No male but me will ever touch you again." I thrust in and out of her again. She feels so perfect. Her body enveloping mine. I never want this to end.

l. I never want this to end. I want him to continue telling me that I'm his forever. I want him to continue to use my name and tell me I'm his wife. "Don't stop."

g. I lean down and kiss her as I continue moving in and out her. An Imperial word for this moment runs through my mind, but I won't use it. With my Lara in these intimate moments, it's only English. I won't taint our moments with Imperial culture. Instead, I say, translating broadly, "You're my true self and I'm yours. It doesn't matter what's happened in our lives to try and separate us. We've found each other and now that the work is done, we can have one another for as long as we both live."

l. Gael kisses me fiercely and thrusts into me more wildly. I move my hips to meet every one of his quick and powerful thrusts. This feels so real and so flawless.

g. When I can't hold myself back any longer, I allow myself to release into her. I feel my semen flowing back onto me as she's so small. When the ecstasy has faded, I lie down next to her and hold her naked body against mine.

l. "I understand now."

g. "What do you understand?"

l. "I could have never left you for Kamos's palace if we would've had this kind of sex in your quarters."

g. I run a finger down her face and then down the rest of her body. "I hoped that was the case, but I wasn't sure. You had no one to compare me to from our species. Sometimes I thought that I should have had you here during that month to make sure you did return."

l. "I did have my moments of doubt about you."

g. "What was it that turned the tide in my favor?"

l. "The way you always have looked at me."

g. "How do I look at you?"

l. "You look at me like I'm free."

Discussion

"He's awakened my body to my humanness."

Thank you for reading, *My Human Wife*. I would like to discuss my inspiration for this book. This book was not easy for me to write and that is because so many of the themes are dark and emotional. I write these discussions in all of my books because every author is inspired to write a book by something.

But first let me mention the structure again, as I indicated in the introduction, some of the chapters are written in duet form for the narrators. Unfortunately, Amazon doesn't allow me to deviate from the text more than a few words, so it was impossible to write a different eBook. I'm sorry for those who were disappointed by the duet chapters. I would encourage you to listen to the audio when it comes out as that is how the book is meant to be presented.

As for the story of *My Human Wife* itself, I was inspired to write this book after reading about human trafficking, watching videos about body count on social media, and seeing *La bohème* at the opera house this past winter.

Human trafficking is horrific. And what's worse is that it's more lucrative than dealing drugs or any other illegal activity. As of last year there were more than 50 million slaves worldwide.

Most would agree, slavery is terrible, but if that's the case, then why is it so rampant across our planet? Why do so many of us turn a blind eye? There are laws in every country against trafficking and slavery, just as there are galactic laws against human slavery in my story, but they are rarely enforced in reality or fiction. As I researched the topic, I realized that there were many factors at play which made it hard to enforce the laws: racism, poverty, immigration laws, Stockholm Syndrome, shame, guilt, social isolation, language barriers, cultural differences, economics, debts, drug abuse, social inequalities, sexism, religion, war, propaganda, and many more issues that make it tough to prosecute criminals and challenging to rescue victims and subsequently reintegrate them into society.

Similar to survivors of trafficking today on Earth, Lara was left with a religious organization, the Fertility Temple, because it had become illegal for humans to be slaves, but at the same time, she could not become a member of galactic society because there were no jobs open to humans and she couldn't be sent back to Earth because she had passed the legal time frame to be returned, so the IGC judge left her at a religious temple. This happens on Earth all the time with rescued victims of trafficking. They are no longer accepted into society so they live with religious groups or victim groups outside of normal society. It's awful to be rescued and freed from captivity only to find out you have no means to support yourself and are not supported by your community.

In *My Human Wife* the Uru abbess lays out the truth for Lara, "This is just a stopgap for the IGC judge until he figures out what to do with you. And my guess is he assumes it'll take you years for a male to pay homage with you which is why he sent you here in the first place. He can't legally kill you and he doesn't want to sell you because now it's against the law, but he's not going to set you free or he would've already done it. And that's why I'm so annoyed. You're going to be with us forever and I never wanted a human pet." The abbess is not unlike many, especially in more conservative areas of the world, who are given the task to look after victims of sex trafficking and rape, many see these victims as having brought the crimes they suffered onto themselves as God's plan, or in Lara's case, the goddesses' will. Given these circumstances, it's not a coincidence that there are elevated rates of suicide, PTSD, and self-harm of survivors after being "rescued" from trafficking. And I am sure Lara would have suffered the same fate if Gael had not come for her.

Lara says of herself at Gala, "I only look healthy on the outside. In my mind, I'm completely disfigured. I'm hardly human at all anymore." And although she also thinks, "*When I was with Gael and when he was kissing me, I was as human as I'd ever been.*" Modern psychology tells us that what happens during childhood development greatly affects who you become as an adult. Lara was abducted and used as a plaything by tentacled aliens. Hela mentions she should speak to a counselor. But Lara knows how to be compliant and knows how to give the appearance of being "okay." In addition, she probably believes her coping mechanisms are enough to see her through life. She has lasted this long. And another key element of her avoiding a counselor is that she might be afraid to open up to how she really feels about something that she is not in control of. At every point, Lara controls her own thoughts and her emotions and that's not something she is willing to hand over to a therapist. Her thoughts and reactions are the one thing she owns (or think she owns).

Throughout *My Human Wife*, Lara is in control of her emotions and how she reacts to her situations at all times, except when she is with Gael. Gael makes her feel things she cannot control. This is love. And love is a strange thing, it makes us trust strangers we just met. It makes us forgive people would we otherwise never forgive. And it makes us do things we would otherwise never do.

And make no mistake, Lara has a good understanding of sex, as she says, "What is sex anyway? Muscle contractions, a bit of bodily fluids." And when she says, "It wasn't rape," at Kamos's palace, of course, she didn't have a choice, but maybe, because of her strange upbringing, she does, in fact, enjoy the physical pleasure of sex, being able to separate her emotions and mind from her physical body. Lara often mentions she goes somewhere else with her mind. Pleasing hormones, dopamine and oxytocin, are released in the body when you orgasm no matter how that orgasm comes about. And if she did enjoy the physical aspects, sex for sex's sake, why should she be punished by anyone's judgement? Or not be believed when she says it wasn't rape? Sex can come in various shades of grey it's not just all rape or blissful sparks of love and pleasure.

Lara knows how different sex feels with someone you are attracted to, as when she's with Gael, "I didn't think Gael touching me, his lips to mine, would feel any differently than tentacled males putting their appendages all over me, but this feels incredibly different. He's awakened my body to my humanness."

It's possible as well that Lara only wants to make Gael feel better about what happened with Kamos so they can move forward with their lives. She says it either out of truth or to put it behind her, or maybe both. But isn't that what people do? Protect those they love by shouldering the burdens of what has happened to them because the past can never be undone and Lara believes she is strong enough to hold this line.

True love accepts many faults. Lara chose to go to Kamos to help others. Gael would not have forced her to go. It was her choice. Just like it was her choice what she told Gael about what happened with Kamos.

Does it matter that Lara has been with so many male aliens? Does it matter whether or not she derived physical, but not emotional satisfaction, from it? On social media this is a heated discussion citing only physical contact, 'body count,' not even the woman's physical satisfaction for each sexual encounter, as a basis for whether a woman, based on how many men she has had sex with (not how many times she has had sex with the same man), should be deemed 'worthy' as a potential mate.

Lara aptly says, "Women have made it [sex] so important because it's a way for the matriarchy to maintain its dominance. Insisting it's the ultimate pleasure to have sex with a woman." I took this idea directly from our own patriarchal society and replaced the word 'patriarchy' with 'matriarchy' and 'men' with 'women.' I do not believe a matriarchy would be anymore just than a patriarchy, it would only be skewed in the opposite direction. Neither system is balanced, but I think it is the human condition to have a power imbalance between the sexes to keep sex/reproduction interesting.

But I digress. It seems some believe sex with an untouched woman, and the only motive in those situations to have sex is *because* the woman *is* untouched, is a kind of magical unicorn moment that has nothing to do with the woman herself, but a conquest of sorts, when in reality it's the exchanging of bodily fluids for sexual physical desire (possibly even one-sided), which is what you see re-enacted in porn over and over again. And it's flat because we know instinctually, it's just sex for sex's sake. Young attractive women will absolutely sell their virginity but there's nothing emotional in that, it's an economical transaction. Just like Lara in Lord Juo's menagerie, all those tentacles were completely transactional for her survival. But she could pretend it was more if that pleased Lord Juo and her audience just like she does at Gala, just like the dolphins at Sea World. They get more fish the more tricks they do.

Sex with someone you have a deep emotional connection to is the unicorn moment, and that emotional connection is not exclusively dependent upon physical body count.

People are all shades of grey and so is sex.

Body count does not matter to Gael. In fact, he's surprised that Lara has never kissed anyone and must lead her in their sexual encounter so it is not completely mechanical and that is *after* he agreed to marry her.

But of course Gael also suffers from an Oedipus complex. Like Lara, Gael had a strange childhood. He was separated from his parents at a young age only to meet them again in adulthood. It's clear, Gael wants to save Lara in the same way he couldn't save his mother.

Lara definitely understands that Gael has issues, but she also recognizes she has issues as well. Gael tells her, "All families are messy in the galaxy." Maybe he is correct? Lara doesn't have the experience to know, (she only knows what she has seen through imported media from Earth what "normal" is supposed to look like on Earth, but many of the women who were also pets tell her what she saw is not accurate). But one thing is certain, Lara loves Gael and we know by the end of the book, it's unconditional love. Gael was not only the first man who kissed her, but he rescued her and is offering her a "good life" in the galaxy that will mean *something*. Lara will be loyal to Gael forever once she makes the decision to keep the child. And Gael finally gets to save his mother by having saved Lara and his half-sibling. Life is messy.

When I compare *My Human Wife* to other stories about body count, especially from the 19th century, like the opera *La bohème* by Giacomo Puccini, I think I have put a positive spin on these realities because despite the high levels of human trafficking now, I believe we are moving forward on these issues. In *La bohème*, Mimì, a prostitute, returns from her wealthy patron to die in her boyfriend, Rodolfo's, arms. Mimì tells Rodolfo that her love for him is her whole life, "Sei il mio amor...e tutta la mia vita," and then she dies. Yes, Mimì, Rodolfo, and all their poor friends lament their dismal lives, but they don't question the system. It's as if it's a universal truth from the 19th century that poor women will be prostitutes and die cold and in poverty.

In *My Human Wife*, Lara and Gael don't give up. They actually fight for what they feel is morally right instead of accepting their fates in the galaxy (Lara must be given the opportunity by Gael, but once she is, she even risks going back to Gala, one of her worst fears, to save others). Gael and Lara risk their lives and their future happiness to prevent others from suffering the way they did. I think it's one of the most noble things a human being can do.

There are many examples of these kinds of noble people in the news and social media today. People who have been through hell and back, rescued from human trafficking, and then go back into those dark places to help others, risking their own happiness and indeed their own lives. I find their stories so moving. There's so much suffering in the world, but unlike in the 19th century where it was more or less accepted poor women be prostitutes, today there are men and women fighting back and trying to make sense of all of this and straighten it out. People risking everything so that in the future sex work will be chosen work and human trafficking will be history.

Many will want to look away from this book just like they want to look away from the atrocities of human trafficking, but if we look away, if we send the survivors out of our societies, then we might as well be like Puccini's characters and condone it as a norm of humanity that will always exist.

And finally about the aliens. In most of my books, humans are mainly bought from galactic traders by aliens who look like humans, their only difference is their grey skin and their advanced technology. My first book, *My Human Pet*, was inspired by the tragic biography of Ota Benga. I was surprised that many readers believe that aliens would respect humans, especially if we shared similar characteristics. I don't believe that is true. We can barely get ourselves to the moon, no spacefaring species would be impressed. I believe we would be treated as lesser beings, no matter how closely we resembled those aliens, not unlike how Americans treated Ota Benga because he was from the Congo and not unlike how we treat people who become victims of trafficking because of all the various reasons I mentioned above.

But because a few people think so highly of humanity, without consulting the rest of the planet (which I really think there should have been a global vote as it affects us all), we have sent our galactic address and all details about ourselves, biology, etc. on golden records traveling onboard two probes, Voyager 1 and Voyager 2 (we have lost contact with Voyager 1). My only guess was that these scientists and politicians in 1977 could never imagine themselves like Ota Benga, Ensley, or Lara. They couldn't imagine themselves being seen as barbaric and lesser by more advanced civilizations, and if we don't get our act together, this will be humanity's downfall (if we don't kill ourselves first through war, AI singularity, or pollution). Alien contact, at best, will be what happened to Lara, Ensley, or Ota Benga, and at worst, our annihilation as a species. I hope no one finds Voyager 1 or 2. I hope as a species we conquer poverty, war, and racism. And most of all stop hating each other. We are all human and all we have is each other in this galaxy.

Also by Olympia Black

My Human Pet

Volunteer 4711

My Wild Pet

Human: A Short Story

My books are available in ebook, audio, and paper.

About the Author

I write science fiction about humanity's relationships with aliens and artificial intelligence. To build my stories, I do not shy away from explicit encounters or highly emotional scenes. My books are not for the faint of heart but are observations about the human condition.

For new releases, please sign up for my newsletter:

https://www.olympiablack.com/contact

With best wishes,

Olympia x

facebook.com/OlympiaLBlack
instagram.com/olympiablacksciencefiction
amazon.com/Olympia-Black/e/B084DLSMJ4
bookbub.com/authors/olympia-black
tiktok.com/@olympiablack_author

Printed in Great Britain
by Amazon

41822106R00106